PASTRIES
AND PROPHECIES

LATTES AND LEVITATION - BOOK 3

CHRISTINE POPE

PASTRIES AND PROPHECIES

Copyright © 2023 by Christine Pope

ISBN: 978-1-946435-61-3

Published by Dark Valentine Press

Cover design by Romancepremades.com.

Ebook formatting by Indie Author Services

CHAPTER 1

Out of the Blue

My best friend Deanne came into the coffee shop that cold February morning looking much more cheerful than anyone had any right to be on such a gray, dank winter day. It had snowed the day before, but the skies hadn't cleared immediately afterward, the way the weather usually behaved in this part of northern New Mexico. No, they'd remained heavy and brooding, threatening more snow but not actually doing much beyond that except making the air feel about ten degrees colder than it really was.

If I wanted to be totally honest with myself, I should have admitted that my own grumpy mood had less to do with the weather and a lot more to do with the unfortunate fact that Max Sullivan, my childhood crush-turned-movie star, was supposed to be back in Las Vegas following a month-long film shoot in Costa Rica. But script changes and other on-set snafus had already extended the production a week beyond the time when it was supposed to wrap up, and now he wasn't sure when he was going to be back in town.

On the surface, this shouldn't have been a huge deal. Delays like that happened in the film industry all the time...or at least, that was my vague impression of how these things often shook out. Max and I had renewed our friendship after his return to our hometown the previous autumn, when he'd bought Sunset Ridge, a sprawling ranch on the east side of Las Vegas, but he didn't like to talk too much about the projects he was working on, some of them because he honestly couldn't break whatever nondisclosure agreement he'd signed, and others because I got the impression he wanted to leave that part of his life behind when he was in New Mexico so he could focus on the here and now.

Anyway, I knew part of my annoyance stemmed from the way I couldn't quite forget that Valentine's Day was approaching fast, and now was only a week off. Absolutely nothing about my relationship with Max could be viewed as anything more than simple friendship, so I knew it was silly to think he'd sweep me off to Santa Fe for a romantic dinner or something if he was actually back in town.

But still....

"You'll never guess!" Deanne exclaimed, and waved an oversized envelope she'd just pulled out of her equally oversized purse.

"You won the latest Powerball?" I asked—a complete joke, since I knew my friend didn't even play the lottery.

She shook her head. "Better."

About all I could do was lift an eyebrow. Deanne was comfortable enough; it wasn't like I could afford to pay her a huge salary as my one and only assistant at Levitation Latte, the coffee shop I'd inherited from my grandmother, but her husband Mike made a good living at his job with the city's community development department. All the same, I found it hard to believe she'd turn up her nose at any stray lottery winnings that might come her way.

Since I didn't respond, only continued to look at her expectantly, she brandished the envelope again and said, "Las Vegas is going to be featured on *Fix My Town!*"

Because I liked to watch home improvement shows when I had some free time, at least I'd actually heard of *Fix My Town*. It was a reality program where the hosts visited small towns across the U.S., places that were in desperate need of revitalization. And because the constraints of filming a reality program meant it wasn't really possible to fix up an entire town—despite the show's title—they tended to focus on three or four special projects that would offer the most bang for the buck, so to speak.

While I might have secretly admitted that Las Vegas had a few rough spots which could use some polishing, I still didn't like the inference that our hometown wasn't perfectly fine just the way it was. "You really think that's necessary?" I asked. "I mean, things seem like they're doing mostly okay around here."

Deanne set the envelope down on the table... taking care to keep it far away from the spot where I was putting together the batter for that morning's batch of cranberry muffins...and crossed her arms. "I thought you'd be more excited about this. I mean, they're going to fix up the movie theater and move a restaurant into the shop down the street that's been empty for years."

True, our one and only movie theater had seen better days and was in desperate need of renovation, and I'd be the first to admit that downtown Las Vegas could use another restaurant. Maybe not fine dining, because that wasn't really the town's style, but a place where you could sit down and get a good meal. It wasn't that we didn't have a couple of restaurants in the area, but they were super-casual pizza and Mexican establishments, and there was definitely a demand for something just a little fancier.

"Okay," I said cautiously. "That sounds like it could be good. But how did the show's producers even find out about Las Vegas in the first place?"

"Oh, Mike and I sent them an audition tape," Deanne said, her expression brightening now that I didn't appear to be offering any further objections to the TV show coming here to spruce up the town. "I mean, we ran the idea past the mayor first, but after he gave the okay, we explained how we'd lived here all our lives and love Las Vegas, and think it has a lot of potential it isn't living up to. But we didn't hear anything for months and months, and then that"—she pointed at the envelope—"showed up yesterday. They'll be here on Thursday."

My eyes widened. "So soon? Shouldn't they be giving us a little more time to get ready?"

"Guess not," she replied, giving a very unconcerned shrug. "It sounds like the production company doesn't want to allow a lot of lead time because they don't want people in the town to try to fix things up before they get here. The show's team wants it to be as natural as possible."

I supposed that made sense. Not that everyone would feel the same way, but I knew several people who would've gone out into the February cold to try painting their fences or doing whatever they could to spruce up their properties so Las Vegas wouldn't look like a complete dump when the episode aired. And even though they'd apparently sprung the news on Deanne and Mike at the last minute, that didn't mean the show's crew and production staff wouldn't have been working hard behind the scenes getting everything ready.

"Okay," I said. This all sounded like it was a done deal, so it wasn't as though offering any further protests would do much good. Besides, I'd completely remodeled Levitation Latte when I inherited it from my grandmother—before I took over the reins, it had been called The Tea Spot and was more of a sandwich kind of place than the coffee shop I'd turned it into—and so I didn't see any reason why the team at *Fix My Town* would have anything to do with me, other than stopping in for a shot of espresso or something. Although Deanne hadn't gone into the details, I had to believe the show's crew would be staying at the Plaza Hotel down the street, since it was one of the few places in Las Vegas that would accommodate a large group descending all at once, and was definitely the most centrally located. "It sounds like fun," I added, since it seemed pretty obvious to me that my friend was expecting more of a response than a single carefully noncommittal word. "But for now, we need to get ready to open."

She seemed to take the hint that I didn't want to talk about the arrival of the TV show's crew, so, even though she looked a little disappointed, she only nodded and went to fetch her apron from the hook off to one side where it always hung.

After all, Las Vegas might be getting its time in the spotlight in a few short days, but in the meantime, we still had a business to run.

I actually had an email from Max waiting for me when I got home from work that day. While he much preferred to text, he was too busy on set to be picking up his phone whenever the mood struck him. Besides, I got the impression that he liked to sit down with his laptop after a hard day's work and write to me, doing something that would take his mind off the movie shoot...which seemed unending at this point...and remind him of the quiet life he had waiting for him back in New Mexico.

Not for the first time, I hoped his latest email might contain the welcome news that they'd finally wrapped and he was on his way home, but no such luck. No, he only wanted to tell me that the next movie he'd be shooting, which was set to start in late April, had now been pushed back to late June, so he'd have more time in town than he'd thought.

I think I'm going to get some horses for the ranch, he wrote. *So if you know anyone who raises horses who's local, let me know. I want real New Mexico horses, not ones from some fancy horse breeder.*

This news cheered me up immensely. Yes, I knew that Max's work required him to be away from Las Vegas for extended periods, but if he was planning on buying some horses, then that must mean he really did intend to make Sunset Ridge his permanent home. He still hadn't sold his house in Bel-Air; it sounded as though his assistant Courtney was living there pretty much full-time now, which I had to admit must be a nice perk, getting to stay rent-free in a multimillion-dollar mansion. Also, now he wouldn't be turning around and basically heading out to yet another movie shoot in less than two months, but would be here for the spring and at least the beginning of the summer.

Assuming his current shoot ever finished, that is.

I wrote back that I'd put the word out about the horses, and finished my email by saying, *Deanne and Mike auditioned Las Vegas for that* Fix My Town *show, and it looks like we were accepted. So, we're going to have another crew here in a couple of days. You may not recognize the place when you get back!*

Then I sent the email, wondering if the producers of the show had decided to come to Las Vegas because they were hoping for a chance...or not so chance, since they knew he lived here...Max Sullivan sighting. If that was the case, they were going to be disappointed when they got here, considering he was currently three thousand miles away.

No, they'd just have to settle for revamping a movie theater whose interior hadn't been touched since the early 1970s, and trying to figure out what kind of restaurant would best suit a space that used to be a western-wear emporium but had been empty for the past ten years. Renovating that particular spot wouldn't be easy, since they'd have to install a whole new kitchen in addition to updating the wiring and plumbing to accommodate that kind of business.

But the old store was big, probably the reason why it had remained unoccupied for so long. The shops here on Bridge Street tended to be much smaller, and therefore affordable for small business owners who couldn't expect to make a profit with that much overhead.

I knew I was lucky; my grandmother Maureen had owned The Tea Spot and the building it occupied outright, and that meant I didn't have to worry about paying a landlord, only keeping up with the property taxes and the utility bills. There was no way in the world I could have paid Deanne what she was currently earning if I'd had to shell out thousands every month in rent or a mortgage on top of my other operating expenses.

Anyway, the cost of redoing the old western wear emporium was the producers of *Fix My Town*'s problem, not mine. For now, I could only hope the film shoot wouldn't interfere with my own business very much. Despite Max's absence these past five weeks, things had been humming along in Las Vegas just fine...and I wanted to make sure they stayed that way.

***

Soon enough, word got out about the TV show's crew coming to town, and everyone else seemed a lot more excited about their arrival than I was. Which made sense, I supposed—Las Vegas wasn't exactly the kind of place that tended to bustle with activity. And even though the production team wasn't supposed to arrive until the next day, things were a lot busier on Wednesday morning than I'd expected them to be, probably because my friends and neighbors and customers were hoping that an advance part of the group might come early to do some scouting or whatever.

"No, I haven't seen anything," I said for what felt like the hundredth time that morning, this time to Lucy Margolis, my neighbor down the street. She didn't come in every day, although she tried to stop in for a latte at least once or twice a week. Still, since she'd just been at the shop the day before, I had to believe she'd only dropped by now because she was hoping to spot some kind of unusual activity in Las Vegas's small downtown. "They told Deanne they'd be here tomorrow."

"Oh, I know," Lucy replied. "But I figured I'd take a look, just in case." She paused there, then added, "Did you know that Bruce and Skyler Mackenzie are the ones who bought the old emporium the *Fix My Town* team is helping to renovate?"

"No, I didn't," I said. That was definitely news to me; the Mackenzies were some of Las Vegas's more prominent residents, and in fact were people I'd planned to talk to regarding Max's wish for some horses for his ranch, since they had a large property of their own to the north of town and bred quarter-horses and pintos. They definitely had the money to buy the emporium, but I'd never heard of them having any desire to go into the restaurant business. "Where'd you hear that?"

"Oh, I bumped into Skyler at Walmart yesterday, and she told me," Lucy replied. "She said it was a project they'd been considering for a while, and then when the *Fix My Town* people reached out to them about taking over the emporium—I guess they talked to someone in real estate here, who told them the Mackenzies had already been thinking about buying the property—it seemed like kind of a no-brainer. After all, Skyler and Bruce had to buy the property on their own, but now they won't have to spend any additional money to fix it up, since the production company is taking care of all that."

On the surface, I had to admit that it sounded like a pretty sweet deal. God knows I'd spent a hefty chunk remodeling the coffee shop and investing in brand-new equipment for the kitchen. I hadn't been able to go top-of-the-line with every-thing, since doing so would have been far beyond my own modest means, but I'd tried to get the most value from every single penny I spent. Honestly, it sounded awfully attractive to have someone else pay for everything.

But what strings would be attached? I'd seen past episodes of the show and knew the designers were careful to make sure any renovations and upgrades fit the flavor of the town where they were working, and yet just because something was fresh and up-to-date didn't necessarily mean it would fit the tastes of the people who owned a particular business. When I overhauled the coffee shop, I'd purposely chosen a warm, kind of funky color scheme—hence the purple couches that occupied one corner of the place—because I knew it would be offbeat but welcoming at the same time. However, I had to believe the show's designers, who'd definitely bought into the current trends of all-white kitchens and sleek quartz countertops, might have had a few choice things to say about my selections.

Well, that kind of tussle would be Skyler and Bruce Mackenzie's problem, not mine. I could sit comfortably off on the sidelines and watch the whole thing go down from a safe distance.

I told Lucy it did seem like a pretty sweet setup, and she nodded and headed out of the shop, latte in hand.

She was the last of our morning-rush customers, and I told Deanne, who'd been hanging off to one side, trying to look like she wasn't listening to Lucy's and my conversation, that she could go ahead and do a quick Walmart run while things were quiet.

"I doubt we're going to have many people in here before lunch," I said. "So you might as well get some shopping done."

"You're sure?" she asked, even as she began untying her apron.

"Absolutely," I replied. "You know Wednesdays are our deadest day of the week, so even if a few people wander in, I can handle it. I know it's a crunch at Walmart trying to go after work."

Looking relieved, Deanne didn't offer any further arguments, but only headed out to the back room, which was a sort of combo kitchen/storeroom, and where we kept our bags in a couple of little cubbies I'd had installed when updating the space. Normally, she would never have tried to duck out in the middle of a workday like this, but she and her husband had had to drive down to Albuquerque over the weekend for a funeral for one of Mike's great-aunts, and she'd run out of time to get her shopping done.

Honestly, I wouldn't have cared if Deanne needed to take off more often than she did. Yes, I was technically her boss, but our friendship was way more important—and a lot older—than our current boss/employee relationship. If we were in a crunch, I might have asked her to wait a little bit, but since foot traffic wouldn't pick up again until closer to lunch, I didn't see the problem.

Because I was the only person in the shop, I went ahead and wiped down the tables and straightened a few chairs that hadn't gotten pushed back in when people left after having their morning cup of coffee. It would have been nice to chat with Tilly, the alley cat I'd been feeding for years and who was now my special charge after I zapped her with the power of speech months earlier, but she was out making her usual rounds of the town. No matter how cold it was, Tilly needed to have her rambles.

I'd tried numerous times to reverse the spell that

had made her start talking, but so far, all my attempts had ended in failure. By this point—nearly four months had passed since I'd gotten the bright idea to make the cat talk so I could pick her brain as to who might have killed Tom Gallegos, our former mayor—Tilly seemed pretty much resigned to her situation. She was careful not to speak in front of anyone who didn't know her secret...which meant everyone except Deanne and Max and me...but otherwise, she hadn't changed her habits much.

However, I was determined to keep trying. Even though she'd stopped complaining about her unwanted power of speech, I knew the cat still wasn't thrilled with me, and who could blame her? Having to watch her every reaction to make sure she didn't say the wrong thing in front of someone who didn't know about her special ability had to be exhausting.

The door to the shop opened, and I looked up from the table I'd been wiping down, wondering if Kyle Isaacs, one of the town's deputies and a former boyfriend of mine who liked to come in and chat when things were slow, had decided to drop in for one of his complimentary lattes and a muffin.

That wasn't Kyle walking through the door, though. I didn't recognize the woman, although something about her seemed strangely familiar, like someone I might have passed on the street several times without knowing their name.

But no...that wasn't it. As she approached, her gaze almost too intent as it met mine, an odd little shiver ran down my spine. Those eyes, big and dark...where had I seen them before?

She paused in front of me and smiled. About my height, with dark hair that had a striking white streak in the front that I guessed was natural, she looked as though she might be in her late forties or early fifties.

"Hello, Skye," she said. "I'm your mother, Alicia Petrucci."

CHAPTER 2

On the List

F or one long, hideous moment, I could only stare back at the strange woman. Part of me wanted to babble that she couldn't possibly be my mother, the woman who'd walked out on my father and me when I was only a few months old, and yet...

...and yet, I somehow knew she was telling the truth. My father hadn't kept any pictures of her around, but I'd found one in his dresser drawer when my grandmother and I were cleaning out his room after he passed away at barely forty. The woman who stood in front of me now looked almost scarily like the image I'd seen in that photograph, as though the intervening twenty-nine years had barely touched her. There was that streak of white in her hair, of course, and a few lines had etched themselves around her big dark eyes—eyes that looked way too much like mine—but otherwise, she seemed to be much the same.

My vocal cords finally decided to unclench. "What are you doing here?" I asked, not caring how abrupt the question sounded. Most people probably would have forgiven me for being a little curt with the woman who'd abandoned me when I was just a baby.

"It was time to come see you," she said simply, sounding as though the last time we'd visited had been only a few weeks earlier, and not nearly thirty years.

"'Time'?" I repeated. "Why now?"

She paused and glanced around, as though she needed to reassure herself that we really were alone in the coffee shop and I didn't have a patron hiding under a table or about to emerge from the bathroom or something. "Because you are coming up on your thirtieth year," she said, "and that is when your magic will truly begin to manifest."

Under other circumstances, I might have laughed at that kind of woo-woo pronouncement. But since I'd graduated a few months earlier from merely reading tea leaves and occasionally having prophetic dreams to casting actual spells...well, all right, one spell and then I'd stopped, since the experience of making Tilly talk had told me I didn't want to get myself—or more innocent cats—in any further trouble...I knew magic was real, even if I wasn't very good at using it.

"What if it's already manifested?" I asked, figuring there wasn't much point in denying something I already knew was true.

Once again, Alicia paused to send a quick glance around the coffee shop, obviously wanting to reassure herself that it was safe to talk here. "Oh, I knew you would have some small skills to start," she said. "Those would have come to you from your father's side of the family. Maureen always liked to talk about her grandmother with the Sight."

Although I'd been doing my best to control my anger at the way Alicia had popped in here out of the blue, the casual way she'd mentioned my grandmother's name made my blood start to boil. Maureen O'Malley had never uttered a single word about being upset or resentful that she'd basically been forced to raise me, considering the way Alicia had checked out after I was born and my father had spent the ten years or so afterward drinking himself into an early grave, but still, I knew there were things my grandmother had wanted to do with her life—like travel now and then—that she'd never been able to do, thanks to having to raise me single-handedly.

"You're angry," Alicia said, her tone candid. She studied my face for a moment, her expression now serious. "And you have every right to be. But I knew I'd left you in safe hands with Maureen, and that it was better for her to raise you than for me to be a part of your life."

About all I could do was set my hands on my hips and stare back at this long-lost mother of mine in disbelief. I'd always thought Alicia Petrucci must be a real piece of work to have abandoned me the way she did, and after meeting her for the first time as an adult, I didn't see any reason to change my mind on the subject.

But even as I opened my mouth to inform her that leaving a newborn behind while blithely assuming her mother-in-law would handle every-thing, the little bell on the front door jangled, telling me I had a customer walking in. A quick glance told me it was Kyle, maybe a bit late for his morning drop-in, but obviously ready for a coffee and a chat.

As usual, his timing was impeccable.

Alicia clearly took the interruption for what it was, saying in an undertone, "I'll come by your place tonight so we can talk more," before she turned away from the counter and headed toward the door, passing Kyle in the process.

Her departure barely earned her more than a quick nod from my ex-boyfriend, which didn't surprise me too much. Like me, he was a native of Las Vegas, and his job as a deputy put him in contact with the public even more than my own line of work did, but at the same time, it wasn't as if he knew every single person in our hometown. Besides, while our little city wasn't nearly as touristy as Santa Fe or Albuquerque, we still got plenty of visitors, many of whom seemed to make it a goal to stop in at Levitation Latte for some coffee to go after seeing the local sights.

Kyle came up to the counter, took a look at my face, and said, "Everything okay?"

"Fine," I replied automatically, and did my best to shift the frown I knew I'd been wearing into an expression that was a little more pleasant. Lord knows I had every reason to be scowling, but I also didn't want to explain myself to him right then. Sooner or later, everyone would find out that my long-lost mother had decided to drop unexpectedly back into my life, because that was just how things worked in Las Vegas, but the longer I could postpone that dreaded moment, the better. "What can I get you?"

For just a second, he hesitated, and I worried that he might try to force the issue by asking some probing questions. Common sense apparently won out, though, because he said, "Oh, a latte and one of those cranberry muffins."

"Coming right up," I told him.

Fetching a cup and getting the latte perfectly foamed distracted me just long enough that I didn't feel as if I still had steam coming out of my ears. All the same, I couldn't help inwardly fuming. Alicia didn't appear to feel guilty at all about the way she'd bailed on my father and me, and had even presumed to invite herself over tonight. The thought lurked at the back of my mind that I should plan not to be at home and see how she liked it when I turned the tables on her...but some part of me was admittedly curious about what she had to say.

Was it really possible that my magic might be on the verge of getting a significant power-up?

"Here you go," I told Kyle as I handed him the latte. "Let me get that muffin for you."

He thanked me for the coffee even as I bent down to fetch a pair of tongs and retrieve the cranberry confection from the display case. Since he didn't seem to be in much of a hurry—probably because early February was a particularly dead time of the year in these parts—I went ahead and set the muffin on a plate rather than slipping it into a bag the way I often did so he could take it to his squad car and get right back to work.

"So," he said, "did you hear about *Fix My Town?*"

Unfortunately, yes, I thought, but I only replied, "Deanne told me about it, and then Lucy let me know about what the Mackenzies plan to do with the old cowboy emporium. Sounds pretty exciting."

"I hope so," he said. "I mean, we could definitely use another restaurant around here."

I nodded. "That's for sure," I said, which was only the truth. Whatever the Mackenzies eventually landed on as the theme for their new restaurant, I knew it wouldn't be any kind of competition for Levitation Latte. My shop occupied a specific niche and didn't offer what most people thought of as "real food," unless you counted my ham and Swiss cheese croissants, which a lot of my customers liked to pick up for a quickie lunch when they didn't have time to go sit down somewhere.

"But I guess we'll have to see how it all works out," Kyle said, then glanced around the shop, his forehead creasing slightly in something that wasn't quite a frown, but close. "Weird thing, though."

I lifted an eyebrow. "What?"

"Well," he said, "this isn't a high-impact show like a movie shoot, but the production company still had to get permits from the police department to let us know where and when they planned to be filming. One of the locations they listed was your coffee shop."

That comment only made me stare at Kyle for a long moment. I'd assumed there would be some spillover, just because the old cowboy emporium was only a few doors down from Levitation Latte, although on the opposite side of the street, and the movie theater was just a couple steps farther along Bridge Street. But Deanne had mentioned only those two locations to me, and nowhere else.

"Well, they'll probably be shooting various places around town for establishing shots and that kind of stuff," I said, glad I sounded cool and unworried...even though doubt had already begun to creep in. After all, just because Deanne had only heard about two projects the design team planned to tackle didn't mean there might not be others. The episodes of the show I'd seen generally focused on two public spaces and one private one, in most cases, the house of someone in the community who'd given a lot to their town and whose home was in desperate need of renovation. "I mean, there were probably a bunch of other places on the list, right?"

Kyle tilted his head, then took a bite of cranberry muffin, as though that would help him with his powers of recall. "Yeah, I think there were about ten," he responded. "Places like the plaza and the hotel, some spots up by the university. Oh, and it looks like they're going to be doing a reno on Pastor Phil's house."

Phil Smothers was the minister at the local Presbyterian church and was one of those people who always seemed to be busy with one project or another, whether it was organizing a youth basket-ball league or setting up a halfway house for women escaping abusive relationships. His home, a small Victorian not much bigger than a cottage, sat on a large, half-overgrown lot a couple of streets over from mine, and while I knew he did his best to keep the place up, a house that old was always a challenge. Having the *Fix My Town* team come in and renovate and update must have seemed like a dream come true.

Honestly, I couldn't think of anyone in town more deserving of that kind of help than Pastor Phil. I'd long stopped going to church by the time he came to take over the Presbyterian congregation when the former minister retired, but he came into Levitation Latte every once in a while for a cup of coffee and to pin up some kind of announcement or another on the bulletin board toward the back of the shop, next to where the bathroom was located. He drank his coffee black and never ordered a muffin, as if he thought the good Lord might frown on that sort of indulgence. Once, I'd tried to tell him his drink was on the house, but he wouldn't hear of it. No, he obviously wanted to make sure he pulled his own weight.

"That's awesome news," I said, and meant it. "And I don't think there's any real significance about having my shop on the shooting list. It just means they'll probably want to come by and get some exterior shots to show how some of the businesses here on Bridge Street have already fixed up their places."

Kyle glanced around the shop and nodded, as if confirming to himself that Levitation Latte truly was shiny and up-to-date, and a worthy representative of Las Vegas. "I can see that," he said, and then helped himself to another bite of muffin, washed down with some latte. "Anyway, it'll be cool to watch the transformations start to happen. I guess the crew will be here for six weeks."

Again, not news to me, since watching the show had already told me that the production team stayed in each location for a month and a half, a span of time necessary to get what were usually some pretty in-depth renovations taken care of before the big reveal day rolled around. "They're staying at the Plaza?" I asked.

"Most of them," he replied, once he'd swallowed the mouthful of coffee he'd just taken. "I guess the two producers are sharing Lorraine Tyler's house, the Airbnb."

At the mention of that particular house, a small tickle of unease wandered its way down my spine. Once upon a time, there hadn't been anything terribly noteworthy about the place, except that it was a stone house which looked like it should be on a postcard rather than rented out as a vacation spot, but last fall, that was where Perry

Lockhart, the director of the movie Max had been filming here, was found shot to death. Suspicion had fallen on Max at first, mostly because he and Perry clearly hadn't gotten along, and for a while, I'd been seriously worried that Max would end up going to jail for a crime he didn't commit.

But tea leaves and a few prophetic dreams had helped guide me to the discovery that Evan Bryant, the husband of Max's high school girlfriend, Raylene, had committed the murder in order to frame Max for the act. Evan was now safely spending life behind bars, and Raylene, with a divorce and a serious makeover under her belt, was now already engaged to Dean Vigil, an attorney who'd moved to Las Vegas from Albuquerque only a few years earlier.

All's well that ends well, I supposed, except some part of me really didn't like the idea of the *Fix My Town* producers staying in a place where someone had died violently only a few months earlier.

"They know about the house's history?" I asked, and Kyle finished off the rest of his cranberry muffin before replying.

"Oh, they know," he said, sounding way too cheerful. Then again, none of that particular tragedy had really touched him, so there was no real reason for him to be somber about the whole thing. "Lorraine had to disclose that information to them when they rented the house. But it sounds like they didn't care, or at least, the news didn't bother them enough to make them back out of the deal. I guess they didn't want to spend six weeks in a hotel."

Even though the Plaza was comfortable and very nicely renovated, I had to admit I probably wouldn't want to stay there for a month and a half, either. For one thing, the historic hotel had its own share of ghosts, or at least was purported to. I'd never encountered any of them myself, but I hadn't stayed there overnight, either. All the same, I definitely got a creepy feeling whenever I went to the lower level where the public bathrooms were located.

"So, the two producers are married?" I asked, thinking that sounded like a cozy arrangement. Getting to work with your spouse every day on what was probably an interesting project sounded as though it would be fun.

Much better than having them disappear to Costa Rica for weeks at a time.

Not that Max was my spouse, or anything close to it. A good friend, and one I was glad to have, even though I hadn't stopped hoping that maybe one day he'd figure out we'd be great as a couple instead of simply as friends.

"Nope," Kyle said, and swallowed the last of his coffee. "Or at least, I don't think so. It sounds like they're just business partners. But shows like this don't have huge budgets like a Hollywood film, so I guess they decided to cut costs instead of renting two separate Airbnbs. The house has two bedrooms, after all."

That's right, it did. I'd never been inside the place, since there wasn't much point in my securing a vacation rental in a town where I already had a perfectly good house, but Deanne and I had looked over the listing one day when we were bored and wanted to see what the inside of the home looked like. Lorraine had done a lot of work restoring the house, which had been built in 1905. It had two bedrooms and two bathrooms, and a gorgeous yard with an outdoor kitchen and carefully planted flowers.

Not that anyone would be barbecuing out there at this time of year. Las Vegas, New Mexico, wasn't exactly known for its skiing, but temperatures around here still got darn cold in January and February. It wouldn't really be comfortable to sit outside until April or maybe even May.

Anyway, because the house had two bedrooms and two bathrooms—as well as a nicely appointed kitchen—it would certainly work for people who didn't have a romantic relationship but needed to be close by each other. Also, while it wasn't the only Airbnb in Las Vegas, it was the one that was closest to downtown, making it extremely convenient for anyone who'd be overseeing a nearby project.

"Right," I said, and didn't bother to add that I hoped they'd have a safer stay there than Perry Lockhart had. No point in borrowing trouble.

Maybe that same thought had passed through Kyle's mind, though, because he didn't look quite as cheery as he had a moment earlier. However, he didn't comment, only pushed the empty plate that had held his muffin and his equally empty coffee cup toward me as he said, "Well, I should probably get going. The chief is okay with us taking breaks when we need to, but she wants to make sure we maintain an adequate presence on the street."

That must have been a new command from Chief DeVargas, because Kyle had never been in much of a hurry to be on his way before this. Maybe she was smarting a little because I'd managed to solve both of the murders that had taken place here in Las Vegas over the past six months, thanks to my tea leaves and whatever higher presence sent those strange dreams to me, the ones that had a definite ring of a truth to them, even if it wasn't always clear right from the beginning.

I told myself Marie DeVargas wasn't the sort of person who'd allow that kind of petty jealousy to enter her mind, but whatever the reason, I wasn't going to keep Kyle from making his rounds...partly because, even though lately he seemed to have given up on trying to get back together with me, there was always the worry in the back of my mind that maybe he'd bring up that troublesome subject at some point.

Never mind that we were much better as friends than we'd ever been as boyfriend and girl-friend...and yes, I definitely recognized the irony of that particular reality, considering the way I couldn't quite let go of the hope that one day I'd have a future with Max Sullivan.

Kyle said goodbye and headed out, and I picked up the plate and cup he'd left behind, and put them in the dishwasher. A quick look at the clock on the wall behind me told me it wasn't quite eleven. Deanne would be back soon, and I had a decision to make.

Should I tell her about the way my long-lost mother had dropped into the shop this morning, or should I let it go and wait to see what Alicia had to say to me tonight? It still annoyed me to no end that my mother thought she could just come by and pick things up as though almost thirty years had never elapsed. And yes, it felt weird to think of her that way when she'd never really been a mother to me, but biologically, I supposed the epithet was accurate.

As soon as the thought went through my head, though, I knew I'd have to tell Deanne what was going on. If she ever found out that I'd tried to hide the way Alicia had come by while she was gone, my best friend would be hurt, and that was the last thing I wanted.

My grandmother used to say that thinking about a person would bring them to you. I didn't know whether that observation was entirely accurate; I'd thought about Max plenty of times over the decade he'd been away in California, and he hadn't returned until just last year.

In this particular case, however, that piece of folk wisdom turned out to be correct, since Deanne came through the door that led into the kitchen/storeroom, took one look at my face, and said, "What's going on? Did something happen?"

No, she wasn't psychic. But we'd known each other since third grade, so by this point, there wasn't a whole lot I could hide from her.

I'd already decided there wasn't much reason to beat around the bush. "My mother came into the shop while you were gone."

My friend's big blue eyes widened even further. "*What?*"

"She just appeared out of nowhere and told me she needed to talk to me about my magic," I said, thinking even as I uttered the words how crazy they sounded. "She said something big is supposed to happen when I turn thirty."

Deanne absorbed that comment for a minute.

At least I didn't have to worry about her saying magic wasn't real, since she'd heard Tilly talk and knew that, even if I didn't consider myself a full-blown witch, I wasn't exactly your garden-variety girl next door, either.

"You don't turn thirty for another six months," she pointed out.

I figured I'd earned a sigh after the shocks of the morning, so I released a breath and said, "I know. But it sounds like she thinks I need to be ready...whatever that means."

My expression must have been more woebegone than ever, because Deanne hurried over and gave me a quick hug. Even that small embrace was enough to make me feel a lot better, telling me that whatever happened with Alicia Petrucci, at least my best friend would always have my back.

And apparently Deanne thought I could also do with a boost of caffeine, because she went over to the coffee pot where it sat on its warmer, poured me a cup, and then doctored it with chocolate and whipped cream, the way I would do sometimes when I'd had a particularly crummy day.

"Here," she said, and put the cup in my hands.

I wrapped my fingers around the heavy mug, glad of how real it felt, how warm and utterly comforting. Although it was too hot to take a sip yet, it smelled heavenly, and I raised it to my nose so

I could inhale a welcome breath of chocolate-scented Italian roast. "Thanks," I said simply.

"It's what I'm here for," Deanne replied. She stopped there for a moment, watching me with her fair brows pulled together. "What are you going to do?"

"Let her speak her piece, I guess," I said. "I mean, I suppose I could have told her to stay away from me, or just not go home tonight so I wouldn't be there when she stopped by, but I guess some part of me wants to hear what she has to say."

Although my friend was one of the sweetest people I'd ever met, right then her blue eyes flashed fire. "Unless she tells you she was kidnapped by aliens and that's why she's been gone for almost thirty years, I don't think any excuse she has to give is going to be acceptable."

Probably not. But while I'd been forced to accept the existence of magic, I didn't believe in space aliens and abductions, so there had to be some other reason why Alicia had decided it was okay for her to remove herself from my life.

And the only way I'd find out what that reason was would be to wait for her to show up at my house and give her a chance to explain herself.

I shrugged, although I was feeling anything but nonchalant right then.

"I suppose we'll just have to see," I said.

CHAPTER 3

Mommy Dearest

Luckily, Deanne didn't press me on the subject of my long-lost mother after that, probably because she could tell I wasn't going to change my mind about seeing Alicia tonight. I distracted my friend by telling her what Kyle had said about the *Fix My Town* crew, and how the coffee shop had somehow ended up on the list of places where they might be shooting.

"Did you know anything about that?" I asked, and Deanne shook her head.

"No. The letter they sent said they'd film various places around town, but if they were going to do any interior shooting in a particular place, they'd let the business owner know." She stopped there, expression considering. "It would be cool if they filmed something in here, but if you haven't heard anything from the production company, then I think they're probably just going to get some shots of the front of the building for some background footage."

I'd already figured it must be something like that, and yet Deanne telling me the production company would have reached out if they wanted to actually come inside helped me relax a little bit. Maybe I wouldn't get my fifteen minutes of fame, but I was just fine with that.

Fame and fortune were definitely more Max's thing.

The rest of the afternoon was uneventful—thank God, since I'd already had enough shocks that day to last me a while—and we closed up at three-thirty as though nothing terribly momentous had occurred just a few hours earlier. While we were walking out to the spaces where our cars were parked behind the building, however, Deanne said, "If Alicia crosses a line at any time, you're totally within your rights to tell her to leave. She's already put you through enough."

"Don't worry," I assured her. "I'm not going to be a doormat. I just want to know what's so important that she showed up now to tell me about it."

For the second time that day, Deanne reached out so she could give me a hug—a kind of awkward one this time, since we'd both donned puffer jackets to prepare ourselves for the short walk in the freezing air. The clouds still hadn't cleared out, and our breath showed in icy little puffs as we spoke.

"Do what you have to," she said. "But you know you can always call me for backup if you need to."

I assured her that wouldn't be necessary, and we both got in our cars and headed toward our respective homes. All the way back to my house, though, my hands were clenched way more tightly around the steering wheel than such a sedate drive should have warranted.

What could Alicia possibly have to say to me? And was I ready to hear it?

I pulled into the driveway and parked in front of the garage, chiding myself for what felt like the thousandth time about getting my grandmother's stuff out of there and either donated or put in storage so I could finally stop parking outside. True, the garage wasn't insulated and didn't exactly provide the best protection from extremes of cold and heat, but at least my old Subaru wouldn't be such a rolling dirt clod if I kept it inside overnight. And although none of my neighbors had reported any problems on our street, there had been a rash of car break-ins around town lately, telling me that leaving my car out overnight might not be the smartest idea.

Well, I'd put the project on my to-do list for when the weather started to warm up.

Because it was a weekday, I hadn't brought Tilly the talking cat home with me. She valued her independence, and although she'd grudgingly agreed to come to the house on weekends, since Levitation Latte was closed Saturday and Sunday and there wouldn't be anyone around to feed her, she'd absolutely put her little black paw down and told me she refused to spend every night at my place.

"I got along just fine on my own until you did this to me," she'd pointed out, sounding irritated, and I'd given up on the idea of having her over all the time.

Just as well. I was feeling frazzled enough that trying to explain Tilly to Alicia—or Alicia to Tilly —wasn't anything I wanted to deal with right then.

No, it was enough for me to wander through the bottom floor of the house and make sure it was fit for company, which of course it was, since I lived alone and generally spent part of every weekend tidying up the place. Clean house, clear mind, my grandmother always used to say, and because I'd been raised to spend an hour or two every Saturday or Sunday cleaning and decluttering, the habit was so ingrained in me by now that I couldn't imagine doing anything else.

Time ticked by, though, and I cast an uneasy glance at the clock on the mantel in the living room as the hour approached six o'clock. What if Alicia's promise to swing by sometime this evening had been just as hollow as her promise to love my father through sickness and health, as long as they both shall live?

Also, to be perfectly practical, I was starting to get hungry but didn't dare throw together a salad or reheat some of the green chile chicken stew I'd made over the weekend, just in case my increasingly unwanted visitor decided to appear the second I started prepping my dinner.

However, the doorbell rang at ten minutes after six, and I ignored the *frisson* of unease that passed over me at the sound, making myself go answer the door as if this was just any regular visitor. After all, hadn't we already gotten past the awkward part this morning when Alicia had appeared out of nowhere, apparently intent on reentering my life?

Maybe so. Or maybe her unexpected visit had only been the prelude to a really big shoe being dropped.

Either way, I knew I couldn't leave her standing out there on the front porch, not when it was already hovering below freezing outside.

I opened the door and arranged what I hoped was a convincing smile on my mouth. "Hi, Alicia," I said. I'd already resolved not to call her "Mom," not when she'd never been a part of my life. "Come on in."

Maybe the faintest shadow crossed her face at the way I'd addressed her. But she didn't hesitate, only replied, "Thank you for letting me come over," as I stepped out of the way so she could enter the living room.

I'd added a coat closet to the entry as part of the remodel, so I asked for her coat and scarf and hat, and she handed them over so I could hang them up. And because—even though this wasn't supposed to be a dinner type of meeting—it still felt weird to not offer food when the hour was so close to dinnertime, I said, "Would you like a snack or something? I've got fresh-baked bread and cheese, or there's some leftover green chile chicken stew."

Her dark eyes—so uncannily like mine—warmed slightly, as if she was amused by the offer. "No, thank you," she said. "But a glass of water would be lovely."

"Coming right up."

Thankful for the distraction, I went back to the kitchen and poured two glasses full from the filter pitcher in the fridge. Maybe my glance strayed to the wine rack sitting on the counter as the thought passed through my mind that this meeting might be helped by a couple of glasses of merlot, but I pushed the idea right out of my head. Whatever Alicia wanted to say, better to hear it while I was cold sober.

When I returned to the living room, she was already sitting down on the sofa. I handed a glass of water to her, then took a seat on one of the armchairs that faced the couch. I definitely didn't feel comfortable sitting next to her, and besides, this way I'd be able to get a better look at her face as she spoke. No, I didn't really know anything about her, but I still hoped I'd be able to pick up something of what was passing through her mind through any betraying expressions she might wear.

"So," I said, doing my best to keep my tone light, "what've you been up to lately?"

Her mouth pursed. Was that a flicker of disappointment in her eyes? Maybe she wasn't thrilled with me for trying to be casual about a situation that was anything but, or maybe she'd been expecting more drama.

Well, I wasn't exactly thrilled with her for bailing out on my father and me, so I supposed that made us even. And since I'd never been the kind of person to make a scene, she'd just have to stay disappointed.

"I've traveled a lot," she said. "New York...Los Angeles...Mexico City...Berlin. I'm not really the type who likes to put down roots."

The words slipped out before I could stop them. "Maybe you should have thought of that before you married Dad and had a baby."

Once again, her mouth compressed, and I

caught a flicker of fire in her dark eyes, carefully lined with smoky shadow and black pencil. Her clothes were simple, a black sweater dress and black boots, but intricate silver earrings glinted behind her long dark hair, almost as long as mine but much more striking, thanks to the streak of white that framed the left side of her face.

"I was meant to be with your father," she said, and her tone was quiet but intense. If she was angry with me, it didn't show in her voice. "The magic of his family was the perfect complement to the magic of mine. But I knew from the beginning it wasn't anything that was meant to last. Your father was a good man, but I knew I'd only be with him long enough to have a daughter who would carry on the Petrucci magic."

"Really?" I asked, knowing I sounded a lot less calm than she did. Maybe it was the way she made it seem as if her own family's magic...whatever it might be...was more important than the gifts that had come to me from my O'Malley ancestors. To be honest, until I cast that wacky spell on Tilly to make her talk, I'd had no reason to believe my talents consisted of anything more than my minor gifts of reading tea leaves or sometimes having dreams that came true. "Then maybe you shouldn't have married him. After all, you don't need a marriage license to get pregnant."

The words sounded awfully harsh as they left

my lips, but I knew I would never take them back. Really, if all she'd wanted was an ultra-magical baby, there were much easier ways for her to have achieved that goal rather than making my poor father think theirs was a love for the ages.

Because he had. He'd loved her unreservedly, and after she left, he'd spent the next ten years easing the pain with endless bottles of Jack Daniels. No, he'd never been drunk enough to miss a day of work, but he'd start drinking the second he came home, as if the very sight of the daughter who resembled her mother so much was more painful than he could possibly bear.

"No," Alicia replied, and now I thought I detected a certain tension to her tone, as though she was doing her best to hold back a hasty retort. "In most cases, you don't. But for you to fully share in both the O'Malley and Petrucci magic, you needed to be legitimate."

This was crazy. Why should magic care about the circumstances of a child's birth? Then again, what I knew about the wonderful world of magic could fit in my tiny quarter-cup measuring bowl, so I supposed I should let that little detail go by for now.

"Okay, so I was born a nice legitimate baby, for what it's worth," I said. "So, why was it so important for you to come find me now?"

For the first time, she reached for her glass of

water where it sat on the coffee table, then raised it to her lips and took a sip. "As I told you at the coffee shop, your true powers will emerge when you turn thirty. It was important for me to find you before that day came so you'd know what to expect."

"Are all the Petruccis such late bloomers?" I inquired. "Because I've been reading tea leaves and having weird dreams since I was just a kid."

Now Alicia smiled, but I got the feeling she only did so because otherwise, she would have shot me a fearsome frown. "Yes, the women in our family have always come into their powers later on. This is a good thing, since it allows a witch to have some maturity before she begins to work with her magic."

Was I mature? Honestly, half the time I still felt as though I was a kid just pretending to be an adult, going through the motions of running a business and maintaining a house and voting and paying taxes and doing all the other things a grown-up was supposed to do. God knows there were probably plenty of people who would have told me that my everlasting crush on Max Sullivan wasn't exactly the sort of thing a mature, level-headed woman would continue to cling to.

But my feelings for Max were a deep, dark secret known only to Deanne, so there wasn't really anyone around who could comment on them...thank God.

"What *are* these powers, anyway?" I asked, figuring I could brood over my emotional development later on, when I wasn't having an audience with the woman who'd walked out on me when I was so young. Right now, it seemed as though we needed to get down to the nitty-gritty while we had the chance.

After all, I had no idea when she'd disappear from my life as mysteriously as she'd come.

"They vary from person to person," Alicia replied. "Some of the women in our family are highly skilled at brewing potions, while others are better at casting spells that affect the physical world."

Like the one I'd cast on poor Tilly, who still sounded like a feline version of Janeane Garofalo. By this point, the cat seemed to be resigned to her state, although I kept trying to reverse the spell... with absolutely no luck.

"You, though," Alicia went on before I could reply, "have a unique combination of talents, thanks to your O'Malley blood. It was prophesied long ago that one day a witch would be born to our family who took the best of the Petrucci witches and joined those talents with the strengths of a magical family utterly unlike ours. That's why I came back, Skye. I needed to make sure you would reach your full potential. Without training from another Petrucci witch, you'll never become what those prophecies foretold, will never be able to have command of your magic when you need it most."

Witches and prophecies. It all sounded like the babblings of an utter crackpot, someone who hung out in the fringe-iest of online forums devoted to the occult and the arcane.

But then I thought about the video I'd watched on YouTube, the one from Madame Wanda where she'd proclaimed that we all could tap into the power at the center of our beings, our *chi,* our *mana.* At the time, I'd been skeptical, but after I'd sent a bunch of gourds flying through the air through sheer force of will and then given Tilly the power of speech, I'd been forced to admit there might be something to this whole magic thing after all, something far beyond my previous modest efforts at tea-leaf reading.

Problem was, I didn't have full control of those powers, or I would have already returned the cat to her former nonverbal state. That was why I had a feeling it was important for me to hear everything Alicia had to say.

"So...what?" I said next. "Are you going to set up some kind of Hogwarts thing here in Las Vegas?"

Even as I asked the question, I couldn't help smiling, mostly because my words sounded completely ridiculous. Also, I couldn't help thinking about United World College, which was located in the hills northwest of downtown Las Vegas and was a place that Deanne and I had always referred to as "Hogwarts of the Desert," just because the buildings there looked so much like the school in the Harry Potter movies.

Alicia's mouth lifted in return, although I didn't detect any real amusement in her expression. "No," she replied. "But I want to spend some time with you helping you focus your talents and learn how to control them. A witch who can't control her power is a menace to herself and everyone around her. After that...?" The words trailed off, and she gave an elegant little shrug before once again reaching for her water. "I suppose that'll be up to you. All I can say is that you're destined for greater things than running a coffee shop in Las Vegas, New Mexico."

Was that the faintest hint of derision in her tone? I really didn't want to believe it, but then again, my hometown must have seemed pretty poky to her after spending the last thirty years apparently jet-setting around the globe. How she could afford to do that, I didn't know. Maybe the Petruccis were loaded, or maybe, because she was a witch, she'd been able to cast enough prosperity spells to ensure all her adventures were adequately funded.

Neither my father nor my grandmother had said much to me about my mother's family, except to tell me she was originally from the East Coast somewhere. When I was younger, I'd thought it was simply because they were doing their best to avoid any mention of Alicia at all, but now I had to wonder if it was that she'd said very little to my father about who she was or where she'd come from. Very likely, he hadn't even realized exactly how much she'd been hiding from him.

"I like my coffee shop," I said, knowing I sounded way too defensive. But I'd worked hard to make Levitation Latte what it was, and I was damn proud of how successful the business had turned out to be. No, it would never make me a millionaire, but I was still living a pretty comfortable existence, especially since I didn't have to worry about paying a mortgage or rent on either the shop or the big old farmhouse-style home I'd inherited from my grandmother.

At the same time, though, I couldn't help recalling what Max had said to me at the town's harvest festival back in October, right before we'd stumbled over Mayor Gallegos' body in the corn maze. He'd asked if I thought I was living up to my potential, if I'd never wanted more out of life. At the time, I told him I was perfectly happy and didn't want or need anything more than what I currently had, but now I had to wonder if I'd been entirely truthful with him...or myself. No, I wasn't at all like the actors and directors and producers he worked with in Hollywood, the ones who were always pushing to be the next big thing, but on the other hand, I'd somehow known deep inside that there was more to Skye O'Malley than met the eye.

That thing was, apparently, my unique combination of Petrucci and O'Malley genes. True, my grandmother hadn't had any magic about her at all, and neither had my father, but somehow those gifts had decided to show up in me after being dormant in the O'Malley family for several generations.

To be honest, I wasn't sure if I wanted to be unique. I just wanted to be me.

"Your shop is very nice," Alicia said, now sounding a little too indulgent, as if she'd realized she needed to butter me up in order to make me more cooperative and therefore willing to go along with her plans. "But is it enough?"

"Yes," I returned, my tone firm. Whether I was telling the complete truth was a problem for me to wrestle with another day. For now, I just wanted to make my mother understand where I stood.

For a long moment, she didn't say anything. Then she inclined her head ever so slightly, as if acknowledging there wasn't much point in arguing with me on the subject. "That's fine," she said, her tone turning brisk. "You have a life here. I understand that. At the same time, I want to make sure you're ready for what will come to you when you turn thirty. Is it all right if I come over tomorrow evening so I can start teaching you what you need to know?"

Refusing her outright would have been rude. Besides, I did want to know what she planned to teach me. If nothing else, my lack of success in reversing the spell I'd cast on Tilly told me I still had a lot to learn when it came to working magic. It would be kind of nice if I could get it to cooperate and actually help me and the people I cared about.

"Sure," I replied. "How about six-thirty? I'll make dinner."

"You don't need to do that—" Alicia began, but I shook my head.

"I don't like performing magic on an empty stomach," I said. "And besides, I like cooking for people."

She was quiet for a moment, then nodded, as if she'd guessed it wasn't worth arguing about. Or maybe she was in the mood for a home-cooked meal, especially one prepared by her long-lost daughter. My grandmother had never talked much about her relationship with her daughter-in-law, for obvious reasons, but surely she must have made dinner for my parents at some point. It didn't seem too hard to believe that Alicia might want to find out if I'd inherited my Grandma Maureen's cooking skills.

"Where are you staying?" I asked next, figuring it couldn't hurt to shift the conversation to the sort of harmless small talk any two relatives might share after not seeing one another for some time.

"At the Castañeda," Alicia said, and there was a subtle relaxation to her posture as she sat there on the couch, an acknowledgment that I wasn't going to fight her on the important stuff, and therefore she could volunteer any information she deemed harmless. "The Plaza Hotel was completely booked."

"Because of the TV crew coming tomorrow," I supplied. "They're filming a reality show here in Las Vegas."

"Oh, that sounds interesting," she said.

Well, "interesting" was one word for it. I could think of a few others, but honestly, I'd been so preoccupied with Alicia's arrival in Las Vegas that I hadn't allowed myself much time to worry about what the *Fix My Town* people might get up to after they came to town the next day.

"Anyway," she went on, "The Castañeda is lovely, if not as close to the town center as I might have liked. I'll just do a little sightseeing tomorrow and reacquaint myself with the area, and then I'll come by at six-thirty."

At least it seemed as though she was ready to

keep herself amused until I was safely off work and ready to begin my magical training, whatever that might entail. She could have come by even earlier than our arranged time, since the shop closed at three-thirty every day, but I didn't bother to push the issue. No, it was probably better for me to have a little decompression time before she arrived, especially since I'd have to make something for dinner.

I asked if she had any dietary allergies or sensitivities, and she shook her head. "No, I'm open to whatever you want to make," she replied. "I'm sure it will be delicious."

And then she got up from the couch, promising again to be back the next day at six-thirty, and I rose as well so I could fetch her coat from the closet and then walk her to the door. I waited on the porch as she descended the steps, doing my best to ignore the freezing air that wanted to rush into the house, and watched as she made her way to a shiny white BMW sedan parked at the curb.

Not the sort of car you generally saw in Las Vegas, which trended toward pickup trucks and SUVs, or even all-wheel-drive Subarus like the fifteen-year-old relic parked in my driveway. What she thought of my current set of wheels, I probably didn't want to know.

Not that she even looked toward the drive as she walked down the front path. No, she got in behind the wheel of her luxury car and pulled away from the curb, heading east toward the Hotel Castañeda.

I realized she hadn't told me how long she planned to be in town. Maybe the duration of her stay depended entirely on how quickly I picked up all this magic stuff.

It was too cold to stand there with the door open any longer, and besides, Alicia's white BMW had already disappeared around the corner. I closed the door and turned back toward the living room. The familiar surroundings should have comforted me, but a chill that had nothing to do with the frigid night air moved its way down my spine.

Exactly what had I just gotten myself into?

CHAPTER 4

Justin Time

Naturally, Deanne wanted to know all about my conversation with Alicia the night before. We stood in the kitchen at the coffee shop while I poured the batter for that morning's batch of blueberry muffins, in surroundings that felt infinitely comforting to me right then. I hadn't slept well, fretting about what the coming day's magical tutoring might entail, worried that either I'd turn out to be an actual dud when it came to magic-making...or that maybe I'd prove the prophesies true, and would turn out to be a witch who could equal Hermione Granger when it came to casting spells.

Neither prospect seemed all that comforting. I just wanted to be the same me I'd always been, no more, no less.

Or at least, a me who could control her magic and wouldn't be a danger to everyone around her.

"I can't believe you're making dinner for her," Deanne remarked, blue eyes narrowed.

"Well, I'm not going to cast spells on an empty stomach," I returned. I'd already decided to make chicken pot pie, partly because I was really good at it, and partly because it was a simple one-dish meal that wouldn't require me to do much more except put together a salad to accompany it. Also, if Alicia announced that we couldn't have wine with dinner because alcohol would interfere with our magic-making, chicken pot pie was the sort of dish that didn't require a good vintage the way a pair of perfectly pan-seared steaks might have.

Deanne appeared to consider my remark, then gave the barest of shrugs. I could tell she thought I was playing way too nice with Alicia, and maybe I was. Still, if there was even the barest chance that she could really show me how to use magic in a way that was at all effective, it seemed to me that I might as well go along for now and see what happened. It would be nice to think of my magic as a useful tool and not something to be wary of.

"All right," Deanne said, after a pause of a long enough duration that I knew it was her way of signaling me she didn't approve of the scheme but also wasn't going to argue with me about it. She'd had a perfectly normal, happy childhood, with parents who were supportive and loving, and who'd just celebrated their thirty-fifth wedding anniversary, and so she'd probably realized she didn't have the frame of reference to really understand my fraught relationship with my mother. "Anyway," she went on, clearly ready to change the subject, "I saw a bunch of cars and trucks and cargo vans heading into town when I was driving in today, so it looks like the team from *Fix My Town* is here."

I wondered where they were going to park all those vehicles. The hotel didn't have a dedicated lot; guests left their cars in any available spaces around the plaza and then trundled their luggage inside, which could be less than fun when the weather was inclement.

But the lot at the police station always had a few extra spaces open and wasn't far from the Plaza Hotel, and there were also other parking lots scattered around nearby where the production company could probably rent some extra space as well. Besides, while the two main construction sites —the theater and the old cowboy emporium— were located on Bridge Street, Pastor Phil's house was a quarter-mile away from the main base of operations, and I assumed the people and vehicles dedicated to that part of Las Vegas's restoration would keep their work trucks and vans there during the day. Probably, his neighbors weren't too thrilled about having that kind of horde descending on the street, but the town's parking regulations were so lax I doubted they'd be able to do much about it.

"Any idea where they're going to start first?" I asked, and Deanne shook her head.

"Not really. Mike says they're keeping their plans as much under wraps as they can."

Which didn't seem to be very much, considering how the majority of Las Vegas's population already had a pretty good idea of what the *Fix My Town* team was planning to do. But I hadn't heard a lot about what their exact plan of action would be, so I supposed there was still a small element of surprise involved.

"Well," I said as I set my bowl of muffin ingredients under the big mixer that waited nearby, "I guess we'll find out soon enough."

It actually wasn't too long after Levitation Latte opened for business that I heard exactly where the majority of the TV crew had headed—right down the street to the former cowboy emporium, which I supposed made sense. After all, it was going to need a lot more work to turn it into a restaurant than the minor glow-up the movie theater required.

"I heard it was going to be a smokehouse kind of place," Kyle confided in me as I handed him that morning's brew—mocha java—and Deanne hovered nearby, not wanting to miss a single tidbit. "You know—smoked meat, ribs, burgers. Sounds like it's going to be really good."

Las Vegas didn't have a restaurant like that, so I had to admit the smokehouse theme was probably going to be a hit with the locals. "Who told you that?" I asked. After all, there didn't seem to be too much point in getting my hopes up if this was an unfounded rumor and nothing more.

"One of the P.A.s who was helping unload a van," Kyle replied. "She probably figured it was safe to talk to a cop."

I guessed so. I also had to wonder if the P.A. would have been so loose-lipped if she'd realized the cop in question was going to hurry right down the street so he could deliver the news to his former girlfriend.

Then again, these weren't state secrets we were talking about, or the plot of the newest Marvel movie or something. Once the *Fix My Town* team really got to work, their plans for the old cowboy emporium would spread across Las Vegas soon enough anyway.

"Can I have one of those maple-bacon muffins?" Kyle asked next, sending a hopeful glance toward the pastries in the display case. I'd introduced the flavor around the holidays, and it had become such a hit that I'd continued to offer the muffins through the winter. Usually, they were gone within a half-hour of the coffee shop opening its doors, but because he'd come in earlier than usual today, he finally had a chance to snag one.

Repressing a grin, I reached in the case and got out one of the muffins, then put it in a bag. Sometimes Kyle ate here in the shop and sometimes he got his stuff to go, but since he was here at a time that wasn't his usual midmorning break, he probably wanted to get going before anyone noticed he wasn't out driving his beat the way he was supposed to. "Anything else?" I asked, knowing my tone was a little arch.

Kyle had the grace to look just slightly embarrassed. "No, that'll do it," he said, and took the bag. "Thanks for the muffin and coffee."

"Oh, you're welcome," I replied. At least he'd finally stopped trying to pay for his treats. I regarded giving them to him—or to anyone else on the police force, or the local fire department—as part of my civic duty, so I definitely didn't expect payment for the goodies I handed out. And, to be fair, Kyle was the only one who took advantage of the little perk on a regular basis. That was partly because Las Vegas's small downtown and the neighborhoods immediately surrounding it were his usual beat...and, I guessed, partly because if anything of any real significance was going on in the area, it was probably happening nearby.

A nod at Deanne, and then he headed outside, where I spied his police cruiser parked at the curb. At that hour of the morning, none of the other businesses on the street were open, so it wasn't as if he'd had to compete with hordes of shoppers and tourists to get a prime spot.

"It would be nice to have a smokehouse here," Deanne said, her tone wistful. "I love The Ranch House in Santa Fe."

I'd never eaten at the establishment she'd just mentioned, since most of the times I went to our state's capital city, I headed straight for downtown and the Plaza, figuring if I was going to play tourist, I might as well go whole hog. But my best friend and her husband made the trip a lot more frequently than I did and had done much more exploring in the area, so they had personal experiences of places I'd only heard about secondhand.

"Yes, it would," I replied, even as I hoped that Skyler and Bruce Mackenzie would hire someone who really knew what they were doing to supervise the kitchen in their new eatery. Smoked food was generally great, but a person without a lot of experience preparing it could be a recipe for disaster.

We had more customers come in after that, and the next hour was busy enough that Deanne and I didn't have a lot of time left over for chatting. The morning rush had just begun to slow down a little after nine-thirty when a pair of strangers entered the coffee shop.

I guessed right away that they must be with the *Fix My Town* crew, since the man carried a clipboard, and both of them seemed a lot brisker and more businesslike than someone who might have stopped in Las Vegas to see what there was of the local sights before moving on to Denver or Santa Fe or Albuquerque, depending on what direction they were headed.

The newcomers both looked like they were probably six or seven years older than Deanne and me, and so in their middle thirties, the woman thin and blonde and intense, in a puffer coat over skinny jeans and ankle boots, the man with medium brown hair and a wide, friendly smile.

"Hi," he said as he approached the counter. "I'm Justin Hale, and this is Jessica Rosenthal. We're the producers of *Fix My Town*."

"Nice to meet you," I replied, and shook the hand he'd extended toward me. "I'm Skye O'Malley, and this is Deanne Daniels."

Justin shook Deanne's hand as well, but almost at once, his gaze returned to me. Something in his expression seemed just on the edge of admiring, although I told myself I was probably just imagining things. It wasn't as though I was exactly looking my best that morning, not with my heavy dark hair pulled back into a plain ponytail and just a flick of mascara on my lashes and some tinted lip balm to keep me from looking completely like one of the walking dead.

Jessica didn't seem as interested in the niceties, because she only inclined her head toward me before she turned around to survey the interior of the coffee shop, hands on her slender hips and her brown eyes slightly narrowed.

Then she nodded and said, "Yes, I think this will work."

Although I had no idea what she was talking about, I didn't think I liked the sound of those words. "Work for what?" I inquired, even as Deanne crossed her arms and lifted an eyebrow. Like me, she seemed to realize something was up.

Justin appeared almost apologetic. "Oh, we want to feature your coffee shop on the show," he replied with a smile that made the gloomy Thursday morning feel almost summer-bright.

But I was used to Max Sullivan's smiles, and they were even brighter than Justin's. Now it was my turn to cross my arms as I replied, "You mean as background color?"

Looking impatient, Jessica Rosenthal approached the counter. "No," she said crisply. "That's not what 'feature' means. We want to make over your coffee shop along with the other projects we're working on here in Las Vegas."

I couldn't quite keep myself from frowning. Why in the world would they think Levitation Latte needed a remodel? Everything had been done a few years earlier, so there was no reason anything here needed to be touched.

Before I could open my mouth to utter a protest, Justin said—still wearing that bright smile, as though he hoped it might help to soften the blow of such a surprise, "It's a new element we've added to the show this season. We have the regular projects—in the case of Las Vegas, the remodel of the movie theater and the complete overhaul of the emporium down the street, plus the pastor's house —but then we'll also surprise another local business by giving them a complete makeover."

Well, I was surprised, all right...and not in a good way.

However, because Justin was looking all friendly and earnest and yet utterly misguided, like someone who thought their quiet friend would enjoy a surprise birthday party, I did my best to keep my tone pleasant as I said, "That sounds like a fun addition to the show. But I really think there are lots of other businesses in town who'd benefit a lot more from that kind of makeover. You see, I completely redid the coffee shop and rebranded everything a few years ago, so there's really no need for you to do anything here."

His expression fell. Even as he opened his

mouth to speak, though, Jessica sent me a slitted stare and said, "Oh, I'm afraid that's not possible. We've already drawn up all our plans and ordered supplies based on the needs of your business. We can't just turn around and try to use them somewhere else."

About all I could do was stare back at her in consternation. How in the world had she managed to get the dimensions of the space Levitation Latte occupied so the team could purchase the correct amount of flooring and all the other items they needed?

For just the barest second, I wondered if Deanne had somehow sent them that information behind my back in a misguided attempt to get more publicity for the coffee shop. But since she was looking just as flabbergasted as I was, I realized she didn't have any more idea about what was going on than I did.

No, the show must have sent someone here to scout the place, someone who'd posed as a customer so I wouldn't suspect them of anything more than maybe hanging out and nursing a latte for longer than was strictly necessary. Deanne and I were definitely busy enough at times that neither one of us might have noticed a stranger taking snaps of the place with their phone, and I supposed there was also probably some way they'd managed to walk around the space and get enough measurements to make ordering materials not too difficult.

Problem was, I didn't want Levitation Latte redone. It suited me just fine.

"Well, I'm afraid you'll have to use those materials somewhere else," I said, still doing my best to keep my voice calm and even, despite the way I bristled inside at the presumption that my beloved coffee shop needed any kind of fixing. "I wasn't consulted on this, and I don't want any part of it."

"Everyone in town loves Levitation Latte," Deanne chimed in, and Jessica Rosenthal sent her a poisonous glare before returning her attention to me.

"You're really turning down a hundred-thou-sand-dollar makeover?" she demanded.

My eyes widened a bit before I could clamp down on my reaction. The remodel I'd performed a few years earlier hadn't been cheap, but it hadn't cost anywhere near that much. What kind of high-end stuff were they planning to install?

But principles were involved here, so I wouldn't let myself back down. "Yes, I am," I said. "I guess I can see how putting some kind of 'sur-prise' in your show is great for ratings, but I'm really not interested."

Justin spoke quickly then, obviously wanting to forestall his co-producer before she could say anything that might get my hackles up any more than she already had. "I'm sure we can work something out here," he said, keeping his gaze fixed on me, as though he hoped his friendly hazel eyes might do the trick when dangling a carrot of a hundred thousand dollars' worth of upgrades clearly wasn't working. "Jessica, we have that meeting with Ben Fredricks coming up at ten. Why don't you go ahead and talk to him, and I'll see what I can work out with Skye here?"

For a moment, she hesitated, every taut line of her slim body telling me she wasn't sure she was on board with that plan. But then she took another look at Deanne and me, probably guessing from our posture that we really didn't want to hear anything more from her.

"Fine," she snapped, then stalked out of the coffee shop, letting the door bang behind her like a sulky teenager doing a particularly epic flounce.

At least Justin had the grace to look embarrassed by his colleague's behavior. "Really, let's talk about this," he said, and his gaze moved to one of the shop's empty tables. "Just give me five minutes."

I seriously doubted that five minutes would be enough to get me to change my mind, but since he'd at least gotten Jessica Rosenthal out of my hair for the time being, I decided I should give him that much. "Okay," I said. "Five minutes." A pause as I figured I might as well offer some hospitality, and I added, "Would you like some coffee?"

"That would be great," he replied, the relief in his voice so obvious that I couldn't help smiling a little. "Black, please."

Even though I hadn't said anything to her, Deanne hurried over to the pot of mocha java that sat on its warming plate and poured a big cup. Murmuring a thank-you, I took it from her and headed over to the empty table Justin had been eyeing a moment earlier.

He sat down across from me. I pushed the mug of mocha java toward him.

"There you go."

"Thanks." After allowing himself a sip, he gave an approving nod. "That's great."

I acknowledged the compliment by inclining my head ever so slightly. "You can say whatever you want," I told him. "But I really don't want to change a thing about this place."

He absorbed the words and then looked around, clearly taking in the friendly mishmash of new and antique furniture, the local art hanging on the walls, the expanse of exposed brick behind the counter with its adornment of floating shelves that held antique coffee and cocoa tins, as well as various mugs and vases. "It's a lot of fun," he allowed. "Still, we can make it light and bright, more modern."

"I live in a hundred-year-old house," I returned. "I'm not really into modern."

He grinned at that response, a grin which showed the flash of a dimple in one cheek. Yes, he really was cute, in a friendly, unassuming sort of way. He definitely didn't give off a flashy Hollywood vibe, but then again, even I knew that a lot of home improvement shows weren't based in L.A. "All right, how about 'contemporary'?" he asked, then swallowed some more of his coffee.

"How much research did you guys actually *do* on Las Vegas before you came here?" I said. "We're not exactly what you could call cutting edge."

A slight tilt of his head acknowledged my remark, although it seemed obvious he wasn't quite ready to admit to defeat. "Maybe not, but there's nothing wrong with making things a little more up-to-date," he told me. "You know, that hundred-K makeover includes all new kitchen equipment."

Okay, he was a slicker negotiator than I might have assumed on first glance. There wasn't anything about the customer-facing part of the shop I would have changed, but I had to admit that when I was buying the ovens and various assorted kitchen appliances and other equipment, I'd had to choose what I viewed as second-tier stuff because I simply couldn't afford anything truly top-of-the-line. Most likely, none of my customers would have noticed the difference in my product, because I could make it work even if baking in an ancient Kenmore, but some bells and whistles were lacking that would have made my life a lot easier.

"Then how about you just redo the kitchen for half the cost, and leave this part of the shop alone?" I suggested.

Justin shook his head and sat back in his chair, although the half smile he wore seemed to signal he respected the boldness of my suggestion. "That won't work, unfortunately," he said. "Viewers want to see a whole place redone, not just the kitchen."

"Then I guess we're back to square one," I replied. "I like my shop, and so do my customers. They don't need white quartz counters and shiplap and faux macrame hanging on the wall."

That comment got me an outright grin. "It sounds like you've watched a lot of home improvement shows."

"Enough," I admitted. "And I won't say I didn't do some of that very same stuff when I updated my house a few years ago. But that was my house, not a public space. I want Levitation Latte to feel warm and cozy, the kind of place where people are comfortable hanging out for as long as they need. I don't want it to look like a model home or something out of a magazine."

For a long moment, he was silent, as though weighing whether there was anything else he might say to change my mind. Then his shoulders lifted, and he said with a smile, "Fair enough. I'll talk to Jessica and see if there's something else we can work out. But...."

The word trailed off there, and he paused, now looking almost diffident.

"But what?" I prompted, worried that he might have come up with a new way of importuning me to turn the coffee shop into some kind of whitewashed beachy retreat and not the comfy hangout I'd envisioned.

"But would you have dinner with me tonight?" he asked. "I'd love to try one of the local places."

For a second, I could only stare back at him. Was Justin Hale asking me out on a date, or did he think buying me dinner was simply a good way to absorb some local color?

Luckily, my brain kicked in before I could say anything too stupid. "I'm sorry," I said, remembering that Alicia was coming to the house tonight to teach me magic. "But I already have plans."

His hopeful expression slipped...but only for a second or two. "What about tomorrow night?"

Good question. Alicia hadn't said anything about getting together after our meeting tonight, although she'd given me the impression that she planned to keep seeing me until she was sure I had enough of a handle on my magic that I wouldn't embarrass the Petrucci clan when I turned thirty and finally came into my powers....whatever that was supposed to mean.

Still, we didn't have any concrete plans, which meant I was free, at least technically.

What about Max? I thought next, and wanted to shake my head at myself. *What about him?* I retorted mentally. *You're not seeing each other. You're just friends. Justin's cute, and obviously interested in you.*

Or maybe not. Maybe he thought taking me out to dinner at The Skillet or the restaurant at the Plaza Hotel was all he needed to do to cajole me into surrendering Levitation Latte to his shiplap-wielding designers.

"I don't know...." I began, and he spoke up immediately.

"I promise I won't talk to you about your shop," he said. "I'd just like a chance to take you out to dinner."

Well....

"You promise?" I replied, and he nodded.

"Scout's honor," he said. "Not that I was a Boy Scout or anything, but you know what I mean."

That seemed to settle it. And even though I might have felt a twinge at agreeing to a date—it felt like a betrayal of Max, despite our friends-only status and despite the obvious fact that I'd dated several people during the years he'd been away—I told myself I needed to branch out a little. Justin was attractive and seemed nice enough, and we'd be having dinner somewhere local, in a place where I probably knew most of the people working there and where I'd certainly have backup if he pulled a Jekyll and Hyde and got all grabby or whatever.

"Okay," I said. "Tomorrow at seven?"

"Meet me at The Castañeda?" he replied, telling me he knew I wasn't going to give out my home address to someone who was almost a stranger.

Then again, for all I knew, he already knew where I lived. The production company would have done its research on Levitation Latte before making their offer, and my personal information wouldn't have been too hard to find.

But at least it looked as though he wanted to give the impression of playing by the rules, so I'd play along as well.

"See you there," I said...and hoped I hadn't just sealed my doom.

CHAPTER 5

Spelling It Out

Rather than being disappointed that I apparently was going to fraternize with the enemy, Deanne was all too approving of my date with Justin.

"It's good for you to get out more," she said as she swished out the coffee mug he'd left behind, prepping it for loading in the dishwasher. "And he's cute."

I couldn't deny that statement, not when he looked like Paul Rudd's younger, just slightly less attractive brother. Definitely not as flashy as Max, but that was probably a good thing.

"It's just dinner," I said. "He probably wants to pick my brain about Las Vegas. Anyway, it's not as if he's in town permanently. Once they're done with the shoot, they'll be on their way and out of our lives."

Deanne didn't appear too dissuaded by that argument. "That's what you said about Max," she replied serenely. "And he ended up buying a house here. Never say never."

I thought that sounded like a heck of a long shot, but I didn't bother to argue with her. No, I only shrugged and headed over to the Breville so I could brew up another batch of espresso in anticipation of the lunch rush.

Maybe Justin Hale was completely smitten with me, or maybe he was just thinking of a way to pass the time while he was here in Las Vegas. Right now, I had much bigger problems on my hands.

I glanced at the clock and held back a sigh. Seven hours from now, Alicia Petrucci would be at the house, ready to teach me magic.

She sniffed the air as I let her in and said, "Skye, that smells marvelous."

"It's just chicken pot pie," I replied. "But I thought it would be a fun meal for a cold night."

"'Just chicken pot pie,'" she repeated, and smiled. "It seems very impressive to me, considering I'm the sort of person who can barely manage to boil water."

"You go out to eat a lot?" I asked, taking her coat so I could hang it up in the closet. It was gorgeous, a deep velvety green, with a softness against my fingers that told me the wool must have some cashmere blended in there somewhere. Between the quietly expensive clothing she wore and the car she drove, it seemed pretty clear to me that Alicia Petrucci must be doing very well for herself.

I wouldn't ask the question, though. During my angsty fretting over whether I'd done the right thing by letting her back into my life at all, I'd resolved not to inquire about personal details...or about much of anything, really, except the magic she obviously wanted to teach me. If she wanted to volunteer something, fine, but otherwise, I planned to put all inquiries aside.

Including the one that had been tickling around in the back of my mind but didn't know whether I had the guts to ask.

Was I her only child, or had she gone on to have more candidates for carrying on the Petrucci family's magic?

My first guess would be no, mostly because she definitely didn't act like someone who had kids at home. True, if she'd had another child soon after me, then that person would be in their middle or even late twenties, and therefore out on their own. Still, I didn't get that vibe from her...and I wasn't sure whether I should be relieved or disappointed by what my intuition was telling me. I'd thought of myself as an only child all these years, and didn't know how I'd react to the news that I had a sibling out there somewhere.

"Yes, I go out to eat most of the time," Alicia responded as she followed me into the dining room, where I already had two place settings laid out on the table. "Or takeout, if I'm at home."

The way she'd answered my question seemed to indicate she didn't spend much time there, wherever that home might be. She'd already made it sound as though she lived a globe-trotting sort of existence, so maybe she didn't even have a home base, but only settled into long-term vacation rentals as needed.

"Which is in New York," she said, surprising me. I'd honestly thought she wasn't going to volunteer much information about her personal life. "That's where I grew up, so I decided to go back after I left New Mexico."

She didn't have much of an East Coast accent, which led me to believe that all her travels must have smoothed away most of the clues to her origins. But since I'd vowed to myself not to ask too many questions, I just nodded and said, "That must be fun."

"It's diverting, that's for sure." A pause there, as though she'd thought about adding a few comments regarding New York City's charms and then had decided against it.

I took advantage of that brief break to say, "Why don't you go ahead and sit down? I just need to bring out the salad and the pot pie."

"Do you need any help?"

A common enough gesture of courtesy, but I thought there might be an additional meaning underlying those words in this particular case. Trying to make up for lost time?

"No, I'm good," I said. "Just give me a sec."

Before she could try to offer again, I hurried into the kitchen, where the salad had already been put together and was only waiting for me to drizzle some of my homemade balsamic vinaigrette on top. Likewise, I'd pulled the pie out of the oven to cool about ten minutes before Alicia got here, so it was also ready to go.

Carrying both items into the dining room didn't take very long, so soon enough, I was sitting down at the table, where she'd taken the place to the left of the head of the table. I'd actually intended her to sit at the place of honor but decided it wasn't worth making her switch seats.

We dished salad and pot pie—I'd set out a pitcher of water as well, deciding it was probably better not to consume any alcohol that might interfere with my post-dinner magical lesson, even if it hadn't been expressly prohibited—and Alicia took a bite of the main course first.

"This is amazing," she said. "It looks like Maureen taught you all her secrets."

"As many of them as she could," I replied, even as I told myself that it was perfectly natural for us to be discussing my grandmother, since she was the one who'd raised me and given me her same love for cooking and baking. Alicia's tone had been casual as she made the remark, signaling that it seemed as if the two of them must have gotten along well enough back in the day. To be fair, Grandma Maureen had done her best not to speak ill of her wayward daughter-in-law, probably because she didn't want to be accused of poisoning my mind against my mother.

Not that she'd even needed to make the effort. God knows, I'd been able to build up plenty of resentment on my own.

But—to my surprise—the conversation flowed fairly naturally from there, with Alicia complimenting the remodel of the house and what I'd done with the coffee shop. She hadn't lived here with my father...he'd moved in with Grandma Maureen and sold his own house after it became clear that his wife wasn't coming back...and yet I knew Alicia had been here plenty of times, since my grandmother had made it sound as if the couple came over for dinner several times a week during her pregnancy.

No big shock there, at least if what my mother

had said about her complete lack of cooking ability was at all true.

And then we'd eaten our fill, and Alicia helped me carry the dirty dishes into the kitchen, and even offered to rinse them off and put them in the dishwasher. I almost said that wasn't necessary, but I got the feeling she wanted to help, if only that small bit. And even though my brain told me it was way too little, too late, my heart wanted to appreciate the gesture.

So I stood back and let her handle the task, which took about two minutes. Afterward, she closed the dishwasher door and turned to face me, expression now serious.

"Are you ready?"

I honestly didn't know if I was. Yes, this was much different from trying to get tips on magic from someone on a YouTube video, but at the same time, I found myself worrying that I might not measure up to Alicia's expectations. She seemed to think I carried all sorts of powerful magic within me, and yet I knew from my own personal experience that I wasn't exactly what you could call a world-class practitioner of the magical arts.

Of course you aren't, I scolded myself. *That's why she's here—to show you the way.*

And hope like heck that the way she'd be showing me was one I wanted to follow.

However, expressing the doubts that currently troubled me didn't seem like a very good idea, so I just nodded.

"It's really not that hard," she said with a smile. Once again, I was struck by how much I looked like her, even if my O'Malley blood had given me paler skin and slightly less deep-set eyes. "I can tell your magic has woken up to some extent, or you wouldn't have been able to tap into it the way you already have. The most important thing is to be comfortable with your gifts and to always remember that they're a part of you."

Easy for her to say. She'd been raised knowing about magic her entire life, whereas for me, it was something I'd only stumbled into very recently. Also, she practically exuded confidence and had the air of a woman who'd always been easy in her own skin, while I still hadn't quite shaken off my years of ugly duckling-hood, even if those years were now almost a decade behind me.

But again I did my best to push aside my doubts, and only said, "I'm ready."

Maybe if I repeated those words enough times, I'd actually start to believe them.

Alicia's lips curved very slightly in a Mona Lisa-esque smile, as if she knew I wasn't ready at all. However, she just said, "Well, then. You know how it feels when you take in a deep breath, how the air goes to the very bottom of your ribcage?"

Since that was a sensation I'd experienced more than once when I was in choir in high school, I nodded again. So far, this didn't sound too scary.

"Good," she said. "That's what it's like when you let your magic fill you. Remember, it's already a part of you. All you have to do is breathe it in and out. It's like making sure you have enough breath to support a high note."

Did she somehow know I'd sung in choir once upon a time? I supposed it was possible. She still had said very little about what she'd been doing with her life after leaving New Mexico, and I didn't think it was outside the bounds of possibility that she might have kept tabs on me over the years and therefore knew the correct analogy to use that would make me feel more comfortable about wielding this supposed magic of mine.

"Try it," she urged me.

Well, I was on the spot now. A shiver of something that wasn't quite fear fluttered its way down my back.

No, it was partly anticipation. I also wanted to know what I could do.

Because I already knew what it was like to focus on the magic inside me, I visualized that golden glow at the center of my being, the one that had sent sparkles of warm light along my fingertips and allowed me to set those gourds dancing near the ceiling all those months ago. Now, though, I didn't just imagine that spark of inner fire, but thought of it moving through me, up and out, like the high note in a solo from *Amaal and the Night Visitors* that I'd once gotten to sing my senior year of high school.

Warm light, brilliant as the sun on a summer day, burst out all around me, enclosing me in a halo of almost searing illumination. It didn't burn, although I had to squint to keep myself from being blinded.

"Wonderful!" came Alicia's voice. I couldn't exactly see her through the glow, but I knew she was still standing a few feet away. "It's just like I thought—you have the true Petrucci gift. Now you just need to focus it. What would you like your magic to do?"

Good question. The house was clean and the kitchen tidied up, or maybe I would've sent a burst of energy all around me to take care of those chores. No gourds on the dining room table at this time of year, either.

But....

Wouldn't it be fun if the name of my coffee shop could be something more than a silly play on words, something that might apply to its owner in real life?

Almost as soon as the thought went through my mind, I found myself floating above the floor, drifting slowly toward the ceiling. No precipitous rush—I didn't think I had to worry about smashing right through the plaster and up into the guest bedroom above us—but still, it was a giddy feeling to know that my magic alone was holding me aloft in complete defiance of the laws of gravity.

And in the next moment, Alicia was floating there with me as well, a proud smile on her full mouth. "Oh, this is fun!" she exclaimed. "I haven't done this in too long."

"So, you can fly, too?" I asked, and her grin only broadened.

"Well, technically, we're just floating. This is flying."

And she spread her arms and went zooming toward the living room, zigzagging to avoid the ceiling-mounted light fixtures. For just a second, I hesitated, then spread my arms wide as well, like a kid playing airplane...only this time, I truly was flying instead of just jumping off a piece of furniture to simulate flight.

I caught up with Alicia where she hovered above the couch, still smiling. "Can all the Petruccis do this?" I asked.

For just a second, her expression sobered slightly. But then she inclined her head a bit and said, "Not everyone. The magic is stronger in some than others. Like I tried to tell you, your magic is very powerful. You can fly...and so much more."

"How much more?" I inquired, simultaneously exhilarated and just the teeniest bit afraid. The prospect of being in possession of quite so many powers suddenly seemed daunting.

"That depends on you," she replied, and began to sink toward the floor.

I followed suit, mostly because it seemed like it would be kind of difficult to continue our conversation with ten feet of height separating us.

As fun as flying had been, it still felt good to have solid ground under my feet, if for no other reason than I wasn't sure how long my magic would actually have kept holding me up in the air. When trying something out for the first time, it was generally better to play it safe.

Alicia's dark eyes twinkled as her gaze met mine. "Do you believe me now about your magic?"

"I suppose I have to," I said. "That was kind of a spectacular demonstration."

"True." She paused there, as if considering what she should say next. "Really, there probably won't be much that's beyond you…if you put your mind to it."

I didn't know whether I liked the sound of that. Yes, playing with my magic had turned out to be a lot more fun than I'd expected, but at the same time, I didn't want to turn into some kind of over-powered superhero or something. I just wanted to be me. After all, it had taken a long time for me to get comfortable with the idea of being Skye O'Malley.

Apparently reading the doubt in my face, Alicia said, "There's nothing that says you have to use your magic on a daily basis...or even at all, if that's your choice. The important thing is knowing how to control it. Otherwise, you could make costly mistakes."

Her comment made me think of poor Tilly, apparently consigned to a lifetime of talking like a human being, even though that was about the last thing she wanted. "If I'm so powerful," I said, "how come I can't reverse the talking spell I cast on the stray cat that hangs around the coffee shop?"

Once again, Alicia's mouth curved in one of those half-smiles. "It's because you cast a spell. Don't you see? Our magic doesn't work that way. It's part of us. You tried to shoehorn it into using a spell because that's how you think magic functions. The magic did what it could, but using it that way is sort of like...." She stopped there, as if casting about for the most accurate analogy. "It would be like trying to use sunlight to power a sailboat. They're entirely different things."

"So...what do I do now?" I asked, now feeling guiltier than ever about what I'd done to Tilly. It was obvious that I shouldn't have started messing around with things I couldn't control. "Is she stuck that way?"

"Very little magic can't be reversed in one way or another," Alicia assured me. "You'll just have to figure out the best way to do it."

She made it sound so simple. Unfortunately, I'd been spending months trying to remove that damn spell, all to no avail.

Then again, maybe my complete lack of success was due to the methods I'd been using, rather than relying on my innate abilities.

"Anyway," she went on briskly, "I think that's enough practice for one night. If you have any questions, you can call me." She stopped there so she could go over to the large Prada bag she'd left sitting on the couch, and got out an expensive-looking silver card case and handed over a business card.

It was very simple, heavy cream card stock with her name and her phone number printed on it. A 212 area code, telling me she really did live in New York...or at least had made sure to get a cell number based in that location.

Any questions? More like a million. But since it seemed pretty clear that she wanted to put a period on the evening—maybe so I'd have some time to ponder what I'd accomplished so far—I only smiled and said, "Thanks for the lesson. It was...illuminating."

"All you needed was the right key to unlock your magic," she replied.

Apparently so. I fetched her coat from the closet, and she shrugged it on and then draped the Prada bag over one shoulder.

"I'll be in touch soon," she said, and was out the door almost as quickly as though she'd teleported from the room.

But she hadn't. I stood in the doorway, and watched her walk down the steps and get into her BMW, just like I'd done the day before. Soon enough, she was gone, and I closed the door.

Magic still thrummed in me, almost eager. Maybe it wanted to play a little more before I settled into something as humdrum as watching TV or reading a book.

I ignored its seductive invitation, though. It was one thing to mess around with this stuff while Alicia was here and could intervene in case something went wrong. Trying to fly—or conjure a million dollars, or at the very least a new car to replace the ancient Subaru that currently sat in the driveway— sounded like tempting fate.

No, better to wait and start with the small stuff. And I knew exactly where I needed to begin.

CHAPTER 6

Cat Got Your Tongue

"You want to do what?" Tilly asked, looking skeptical.

To be fair, I could see why she'd be dubious. I'd been trying to reverse the spell for months, with a singular lack of success. There was absolutely no reason for her to believe I'd finally manage it at last.

"I'm going to try a new way of reversing the spell," I said. "I've made some breakthroughs with my magic, and I think I might finally be able to do it this time."

Her green eyes slitted. She was a big, sleek black cat who looked glossier and healthier than most strays, thanks to the way I'd been feeding her Science Diet exclusively over the past few months as a way of bribing her to only accept food from me. Maybe I was being too cautious, but I just couldn't run the risk of someone overhearing her make a stray remark about any treats she was being offered.

"Well...." The word hung in the air for a moment, and her tail lashed back and forth.

"Well what?" I asked. "I'm really sure this is going to work. I've just been going about it the wrong way."

Once again, Tilly hesitated. She glanced around the storeroom/kitchen where we were holding our convo, but since it was o'dark thirty—that is, not quite a quarter to six—Deanne hadn't come in yet. Not that I thought her presence should be much of an impediment, anyway, since Deanne was in on Tilly's little secret.

At last, the cat released a small hiss and said, "Maybe I don't want to stop talking."

I stared at her, flabbergasted. Ever since I'd cast that damn spell on her, she'd complained about how she hated having to talk like a human and how that, now she could speak, we expected her to act as our spy.

That last bit really wasn't fair, because even though Max and I had hoped to use her as our eyes and ears to help figure out who had killed Tom Gallegos, the former mayor, we certainly hadn't pressed her into service again after it had been revealed that Dave Gallegos, Tom's younger brother, was the murderer. No, Tilly had been allowed to roam around Las Vegas's streets pretty much unfettered, with the only caveat being that she absolutely had to make sure she didn't speak around anyone other than Deanne and Max and me.

"You want to keep talking?" I asked, once I'd found my voice.

Another of those pauses. I could tell she really hated having to confess her true feelings to me, even as she knew she had to tell me the truth or risk losing a power of speech she didn't hate so much after all.

"It's good to be able to talk...sometimes," she said. "But I don't like having to worry about whether or not I might let something slip in front of the wrong person. Is there any way to cast a spell so I only talk in front of you and Max and Deanne, and no one else?"

Good question. That really would be the perfect solution, since Tilly didn't have to hide anything when she was around us. But not being able to speak in the presence of anyone else would allow her to roam more freely, the way she used to, and to take treats from anyone who was willing to offer them. I knew she didn't like having her style cramped, and who could blame her? She'd spend the previous part of her life being able to go wherever she wanted and do whatever she wanted, whenever she wanted. I fed her really well, but clearly, that wasn't enough.

Even so, I was in uncharted territory here. This sounded like a pretty specific kind of magic, one I wasn't sure I could execute with any level of competence or accuracy.

But Alicia seemed to have confidence in me, and I reminded myself that this wouldn't be like casting a spell. No, it would be more along the lines of sending a particular intention out into the universe, one backed by the magic that lived inside me. Framed that way, the task didn't seem quite so daunting.

"Let me see what I can do," I said.

Tilly's tail moved back and forth, indicating she wasn't entirely sure I could do anything at all. But at least she continued to sit where she was and hadn't bolted for the cat door I'd installed next to the back entrance to the building.

I drew in a breath like I had the evening before, remembering what it felt like to have magic infuse that breath, to fill the very center of my being. And I looked down at Tilly, and thought of the way she would talk to me and Deanne and Max, and how I wanted to make sure she wouldn't lose that particular skill. At the same time, I imagined all the other people who had shops and restaurants and galleries along Bridge Street, and all the other residents of Las Vegas who came and went and who might have come into contact with the stray cat. I thought of her going past those people, sleek and graceful and silent, with no reason to talk to any of them.

Golden light flared around Tilly and then was gone as quickly as it had come. Her green eyes widened in alarm, and she demanded, "What did you do?"

"I cast the spell," I said calmly, then shook my head. I really needed to stop thinking of magic in those terms. What I'd just done was the polar opposite of reciting a carefully composed set of words designed to create a particular outcome, so there wasn't any way I could really refer to it as a spell. "Or at least, I made the magic do what I needed it to do. You can talk to me—and to Deanne and Max—but that's it."

Tilly's sleek black head tilted to one side. "How do you know for sure?"

I shrugged and went over to the mixing table, where the neglected ingredients for that morning's various batches of muffins awaited. "Well, you're talking to me right now, so we know one part of it worked. I guess the only way to find out if the whole enchantment was successful would be to go out and try to talk to someone else."

Judging by the way her tail whipped back and forth, she wasn't too thrilled by that suggestion. "Wasn't the whole idea to have me *not* talk around other people?"

"True," I said calmly. "But you can say something neutral like 'how' or something. Anyone who's not paying much attention will probably think you said 'meow.'"

Tilly was silent for a moment, obviously mulling over my proposal. Then she inclined her head ever so slightly. "Okay, that could work. I'll go test it now."

Before I could offer an admonition to be careful, she'd already launched herself across the room and through the cat door. A little shiver of worry went through me.

What if the spell hadn't worked? What if the person listening realized that she'd said a very human word, and hadn't simply uttered some random feline sound?

Well, people seemed to have an infinite capacity for self-delusion, so I had to believe that even if the magic intention I'd just set didn't turn out exactly the way I wanted, anyone hearing Tilly speak a word in English would still believe she'd only meowed or made some other kind of cat-specific sound.

After all, cats couldn't talk, right?

Five minutes passed, and then five more. Deanne came breezing in, took a look at my face, and said, "What's the matter? Did Alicia bail on you last night?"

I shook my head. "No, she was right on time... and taught me some valuable stuff." Briefly, I explained the jump I'd made in my magical skills the evening before, during which my friend's eyes grew wider and wider. Then I explained how I'd just tried to tweak the enchantment that allowed Tilly to talk, adding, "I hope I didn't make a huge mistake, though. She should have been back by now."

At that exact moment, the cat door opened, letting in a short shock of freezing air before it shut again. Tilly crossed the storeroom/kitchen and settled on her haunches in front of me, then announced, "Worked like a charm!"

"It did?" Deanne and I said simultaneously.

The cat's whiskers twitched in what might have been amusement. "Yep. I headed over to Tortilla Street, because I figured Arnie Martinez would be out there early, dumping yesterday's trash. Sure enough, he was out back in the alley. So I said, 'how!' and he didn't even blink. Then I said, 'Hi, Arnie,' and again, he didn't react. That is, he sort of waved at me and said, 'No fish today, kitty,' but that was it. He obviously didn't understand what I was saying."

I didn't sigh in relief, but a little knot of tension between my shoulder blades loosened slightly. It sounded as though the magic really had worked exactly the way it was supposed to.

"That's amazing," Deanne breathed, although I noticed the way she darted a sideways glance at me, as if she half expected me to start glowing with out-of-control magic like the heroine of *WandaVision* or something.

However, I didn't feel any different. Or rather, while I couldn't help being excited at the thought of what else I might do with my magic, I also understood deep down that it wasn't going to develop a mind of its own and start rampaging around Las Vegas, leaving some Avengers-sized destruction in its wake.

At least, I sincerely hoped it wouldn't.

"Well, since I don't have to worry about people hearing me talk, I'm out to wander again," Tilly told us. "Don't expect me back any time soon."

And before either Deanne or I could say anything, the cat had whisked herself across the floor and right out the cat door, letting it bang shut in an emphatic way that seemed to signal she was ready to go back to her old habits.

For a long moment, my friend and I could only stare at each other. Then Deanne said, "So...now what?"

I picked up my bowl full of batter and started pouring it into a nicely greased muffin tin. "Now, we get ready to open."

After all, what else what I was supposed to do? Magic or no, life went on...and people still wanted their coffee and morning pastries.

Maybe it was because the sun had finally decided to make an appearance that morning, or maybe because the town's residents figured Friday morning would be a good time to stroll by and take a look at what was happening down at the old cowboy emporium and then get a coffee while they were at it. Either way, Levitation Latte was positively humming that morning, and I didn't get a chance to really catch my breath and even begin to process everything that had happened over the past twenty-four hours until well past ten-thirty.

And even then, that window of peace and quiet didn't last very long before Alicia came in. She smiled at Deanne and me, and said, "Any muffins left?"

"A few," I replied, glad she'd come here for such a prosaic reason. Yes, Deanne already knew everything that was going on—we'd resolved long ago not to keep secrets from one another—but still, I would rather have kept the magical discussions for another time a little later in the day. "And there are fresh batches of blueberry and maple bacon in the oven, if you don't want cranberry or banana nut."

"Cranberry is fine," Alicia said. "And what's the brew of the day?"

"Italian roast and Sumatran," Deanne supplied.

"Italian roast, please."

My friend hurried off to pour a cup for our latest customer, while I opened the display case and got out one of the roughly half-dozen muffins that had survived the morning rampage. "Is this to go, or did you want to eat here?"

Alicia's gaze moved over the now-empty coffee shop. "Oh, I'll eat here. It's so nice and cozy."

Glad that she apparently approved of my design aesthetic, I went ahead and set a cranberry muffin on a plate. At the same time, Deanne came over with a steaming cup of Italian roast.

"Cream or sugar?"

"None, thank you. I drink it black."

Which didn't surprise me too much. Not that I could claim to be an expert on Alicia Petrucci, but, despite her utter belief in her family's magic—a belief I now had to share, considering I'd spent part of the previous evening flying around the house— she seemed like a very brisk, pragmatic sort of person. I had to wonder if she would have ended up butting heads with my father and leaving eventually anyway, even if she'd stuck around longer than those scant two months after I was born. He'd also been stubborn and down-to-earth, although those qualities hadn't been enough to prevent him from seeking refuge in a bottle after she was gone, and I could see how they might have rubbed each other the wrong way after not too much time together.

Deanne handed Alicia her mug of coffee, and she headed over to the sofa by the window and sat down, apparently content to have her morning shot of caffeine and something sweet and satisfying to go with it.

"She seems...nice," Deanne said to me in an undertone. I detected a hint of surprise in her voice, as though she couldn't imagine how the woman who'd walked out on her newborn child might turn out to be not half bad after all.

I nodded. "I think so. Or at least, it seems to me as though she's making an effort." But because I didn't want to keep discussing my mother when she was sitting only a couple of yards away, I added, "I need to go check on the muffins in the oven."

A knowing expression crossed Deanne's face, but she didn't say anything. The oven back in the kitchen had a timer loud enough that we could hear it going off even when we were out in the coffee shop's public space, so she must have guessed I was using the muffins as an excuse to get away.

And that was fine. I didn't care if my best friend had seen right through the ploy. The important thing was that I was able to go in the back and claim a little time to regain my equilibrium.

Because I had to admit that one part of me was wondering how I could be so casual around Alicia when her leaving had been one of the most traumatic things that had ever happened to me, even if I'd been too young at the time to comprehend what was really going on. But babies grow up, and I was definitely now old enough to understand what having a mother who'd abandoned me had done to my brain and my heart.

I had every right to be angry. Furious, really. But another part of my soul was just really glad that she was here now, that she wanted to make sure she helped unlock my magic.

Well, that had definitely happened. I still had a hard time wrapping my brain around the realization that I'd been able to launch myself into the air the night before using only the powers I'd apparently been born with.

Right then, the timer on the oven went off, giving some credence to the little white lie I'd told Deanne a minute earlier. I grabbed some oven mitts and pulled the trays out of the oven, and set them on the counter. The muffins would need to cool a bit before I could remove them from the tin and take them out to the display case, but at least now I didn't have to worry about running out before we closed at three-thirty.

I was just pulling off one of the oven mitts when I heard a woman's imperious tones through the partially open door that led out to the main part of the shop.

"Where is Skye? I need to talk to her right now!"

At first, that voice didn't sound familiar. I blinked, and realized who it must be out there.

Jessica Rosenthal.

Great. Just great.

Justin had said he would smooth things out with her, but, judging by the angry note in her voice, those "things" were still as lumpy as a batch of rocky road fudge.

I took a moment to gather my composure as best I could, and then I headed out to the counter, where an annoyed-looking Deanne was facing an obviously angry Jessica.

"What's the problem?" I asked in my best customer-service voice.

At once, Jessica rounded on me. "You know exactly what the problem is, Ms. O'Malley. The production company bought supplies to fix up this coffee shop, not some other hole-in-the-wall in this godforsaken town. This isn't one size fits all. We can't take those supplies and use them somewhere else."

The "godforsaken town" remark rankled, as I was sure she'd intended it to. So much for the show's sweetness and light about community togetherness and all that stuff. Clearly—for Jessica Rosenthal, at least—all that talk was for marketing purposes and nothing else.

However, I did my best to control my temper. For one thing, I didn't want her to have the satisfaction of seeing me lose control, and for another, I honestly didn't know what might happen if I really lost it and blew my top. Would my magic decide she was an enemy and try to take her out?

I certainly hoped not. The *Fix My Town* producer was currently at the top of my poop list, but that didn't mean I wanted to see her dead.

No, I just wanted her out of my hair.

"I don't remember signing a contract," I said, hands on my hips. "And because we don't have any kind of signed agreement, I don't owe you a damn thing."

As I was speaking, Alicia approached from behind Jessica. "Skye, what's the matter?"

Great. The last thing I wanted was my mother butting in. I was sure she was only trying to help, but I could handle this on my own. After all, I'd managed without her help for the past twenty-nine years.

"Just a misunderstanding," I began, but Jessica wouldn't let me go any further.

"And who are you?" she demanded, looking the newcomer up and down. Her mouth tightened, and I got the distinct impression that she was actually disappointed Alicia looked so presentable, in yet another of her black sweaters and perfectly fitting jeans, with high-heeled boots and a circle of diamonds winking from the middle finger of her right hand. She definitely didn't look like anyone from Las Vegas, New Mexico, that was for sure.

"I'm Skye's mother," Alicia said imperturbably.

"Oh, so you have to have Mommy come in and fight your battles for you?"

Alicia ignored the other woman's sneer, saying, "No, Skye is completely capable of fighting her own battles. I was just wondering what was so important that you'd come in here and cause such a commotion while people are trying to enjoy their morning coffee."

For a second, Jessica looked almost taken aback by that comment, as though she wasn't quite sure what tack she should take next. But then she gathered herself and said, "Your daughter has been offered a complete makeover of this shop—and a chance for her business to gain exposure on a national cable show— and she's turned it down! Maybe you can talk some sense into her."

Possibly, one of Alicia's eyebrows lifted ever so slightly. She glanced away from Jessica and let her gaze travel around the coffee shop for a moment, then turned back toward the two of us. "I don't see anything that needs remodeling here."

Despite what Alicia had done to me, I couldn't hold back a rush of warmth at hearing those words, at listening to her quiet, steady defense of Levitation Latte. The place meant a lot to me, and I appreciated her approval more than I wanted to admit.

Jessica planted her hands on her hips. She was wearing jeans and boots and a puffer vest, hair pulled back in a ponytail, and I guessed she'd come straight here from one of the other sites the production crew was working on. "It's hopelessly out of date," she said. "It's dark and dingy and not welcoming at all."

My lips parted as I prepared to deliver a retort, but Alicia was faster.

"Oh, and I suppose you want to make it light and bright, paint over that brick, maybe install a little shiplap, make all the cabinets white and hang a few faux macrame pieces on the wall?"

Those words could have come right out of my own mouth, and I couldn't quite hold back a nervous laugh. Jessica's dark eyes shot daggers at me, her mouth tightening further—and accentuating the lines that had already started to dig themselves into the skin around her mouth.

"You think this is a joke?" she demanded.

"No," Alicia said calmly. "But I also think your 'makeover' would turn this place into something that might as well have come out of a cookie cutter. Levitation Latte is unique, just like my daughter. And that means you should really find someone else who'd be happy to have your crew remodel their place."

"I understand what you're trying to do for me," I put in quickly. Part of me wanted to hug Alicia for the way she'd come to my defense, but I had a feeling such a public display of affection would be awkward for both of us…not to mention annoying Jessica Rosenthal that much more. It was probably too late to repair the damage, but I thought I should try anyway. "I just don't think it's what my shop needs right now."

A hideous pause, while Jessica glared at the two of us. Then she snapped, "This isn't the end of this matter," and stalked out of the coffee shop, only pausing to make sure she slammed the door extra hard on her way out.

"I'm sorry," Alicia said, and she actually did look contrite. "I probably shouldn't have butted in like that. It just that that woman has a *very* carrying voice."

"No kidding," Deanne put in. She'd stayed quiet during the drama, obviously guessing that having someone else leap to my defense would only make Jessica Rosenthal that much angrier. "I'm surprised people couldn't hear her all the way down the street."

"Don't be sorry," I told Alicia. "You helped me get rid of her, and that's the important thing."

Whether she'd stay gone was an entirely different question, but I figured I wouldn't worry about that until it happened. For now, it was enough to know my mother had felt compelled to come to my defense, even if I also realized I could have managed just fine on my own.

Maybe.

I managed to put on a smile, and added, "Want me to freshen your coffee?"

The whole rest of the day, I kept thinking I'd get a call from Justin Hale telling me that he needed to cancel our dinner date at the Castañeda's restaurant. I didn't think his co-producer was the sort of person who would hold back and avoid telling him about what had gone down at Levitation Latte that morning...and I also wouldn't put it past her to forbid him to see me.

But I didn't hear anything from him at all, leading me to believe the date was still on. I went home and changed out of my work clothes and into the pretty teal cashmere sweater Deanne had given me for my birthday, along with my best pair of jeans and some ankle boots I'd bought a while back on one of my infrequent trips to Albuquerque. The outfit was nice, but not too fancy, and I hoped it would strike the right note.

Of course, I didn't really know where any of this was going. The *Fix My Town* team would be here for six weeks, but after that, they'd be off to the next location. Even if it turned out that Justin and I had good chemistry, it wasn't as if anything could possibly come of it.

And that had to be for the best. After all, if I was meant to be with Max Sullivan, then I couldn't let things get too serious with Justin, right?

Right.

It didn't help that I had an email from Max waiting for me when I got home. Nothing earth-shattering, just him relating a funny story about how one of the stunt monkeys got loose in the craft service tent and wreaked utter havoc, but still, simply hearing from him was enough to send little pangs of guilt shooting through me.

What if he found out I'd gone out on a date with someone else in his absence?

He wouldn't care, I told myself. *How many dinners with beautiful women do you think he's had since he got to Costa Rica?*

I really didn't want to answer that question, so I pushed it aside. Instead, I applied fresh lip gloss, finger-combed my wavy hair and told myself it looked fashionably tousled rather than just messy, and went downstairs.

The Castañeda Hotel was only about five minutes from my house, so even if it turned out that Justin had ghosted me, it wasn't as if I would have wasted much time going to and from the restaurant.

But no, he was waiting at the bar when I came in, and immediately got up from the stool where he'd been sitting.

"You look great," he said, and I found myself flushing a little.

"Thanks," I managed to reply.

Luckily, the hostess—a girl from my former high school named Tiffany—came over and asked if we'd like to be shown to our table right then, so I didn't have much time to spend on being embarrassed. Instead, I followed her and Justin to a table in one corner, although not one I'd ever shared with Max, thank God.

She handed us menus and told us our server would be by in a minute or so. As soon as she was gone, Justin said, "I am so sorry about Jessica."

I blinked at him. "What?"

His left eyebrow lifted slightly. "She told me how she went to your shop this morning and had it out with you. I'm really sorry about that."

"It's okay," I said automatically, then paused. "That is, I guess it's not *really* okay, but there's only so much she can do, right? It's not like I signed a contract to be on the show."

At once, he looked much more relaxed. "No, you didn't. And I tried to tell her that very same thing—and also that it was totally inappropriate for her to go over there and harangue you like that. Of course, being Jessica, she didn't apologize, only said that I must not care about the success of the show and that I could have fun explaining to the network why we ended up with about forty thousand dollars' worth of materials we couldn't use."

Ouch. Yes, Jessica had said the remodel was worth a hundred grand, but I'd assumed a large chunk of that total was labor. Because I'd had to bargain-hunt when I redecorated the shop myself, I hadn't spent anywhere near that on materials and equipment.

"Can't you return the stuff?" I asked.

"Some of it," Justin replied. "The new oven and espresso machine, sure. But probably not the flooring or the lumber and quartz we got to build you a new counter area."

Double ouch. I told myself not to feel guilty, that none of this was my fault, and yet I hated to see anything go to waste. "You can donate it to Habitat for Humanity and get a nice tax write-off," I said, and now Justin actually smiled.

"That was my thought, but I figure I'll wait a few days for Jessica to cool down before I suggest it."

The waiter came by then and asked if we wanted to order anything to drink. We'd both been so engrossed in our conversation that I hadn't even looked at the menu, but Justin didn't seem as though he'd been caught too off guard.

"Is a bottle of wine okay?" he asked me, and I

nodded. He turned toward the waiter and said, "Then a bottle of the True Myth cabernet."

"Very good," the man said. "I'll be back with your bottle and some glasses in just a minute."

Most of the time, I didn't drink that much with dinner, but I didn't have far to go to get home. Besides, I was still feeling a little frayed after that encounter with Jessica this morning. A glass of wine or two would definitely help to take the edge off.

As we were waiting for the server to come back with our bottle of cab, Justin's phone rang from inside his jacket pocket. He shot me an apologetic look and said, "Sorry—I need to take this."

"That's fine," I replied. Usually, I took a dim view of men answering their phones while we were out on a date, but this was different. Justin was working while here in Las Vegas, and lord only knows what kind of emergency might have cropped up in his absence.

He put the phone to his ear. "Justin Hale."

A silence followed as he listened to the caller. The lighting in the hotel's restaurant wasn't the greatest, but it looked to me as though he'd suddenly gone pale, his features turning pinched with shock.

Then he said, "No, I can be over there in just a couple of minutes. Right. Okay. See you soon."

He returned the phone to his pocket as I stared

across the table at him. I had no idea what was going on, but it sure sounded as though our date was about to end before it even got started.

"What's the matter?" I blurted.

Justin pulled in a breath. His face was still pale, but his gaze met mine squarely.

"That was one of our P.A.s. She went over to the Airbnb where Jessica and I are staying to drop off some release forms." He almost stammered the last word, then stopped again and appeared to do his best to steady himself.

"She found Jessica dead in the living room, strangled with her phone's charging cord."

CHAPTER 7

Bellwether

"I should have warned Jessica Rosenthal that house was unlucky," I said.

Deanne pushed a cup of hot tea into my hand. "None of this is your fault," she replied, then flicked an uneasy glance toward her husband Mike, who hovered uncomfortably nearby. "It's not like Perry Lockhart's death wasn't all over the internet. Lorraine has a disclaimer right on the Airbnb listing so no one's blindsided by the history of that house."

I knew that was true, because a while back, Deanne had looked up the listing and showed me the new verbiage the owner had included, probably because she'd thought I would find it interesting. And because I'd realized a while back that I had a bad habit of blaming myself for things I had nothing to do with, I knew I needed to do my best to take Deanne's advice to heart.

After Justin had gotten that awful phone call, he'd excused himself to go over to the Airbnb. The P.A.—who sounded as though she was pretty young, in her early twenties—had been practically in hysterics, and so it seemed painfully obvious to me that he would have to be the one to call the police and have them come over to investigate the crime scene.

And I, feeling mildly freaked myself, hadn't wanted to go straight home. Instead, I'd called Deanne and told her an emergency had come up and I really wanted to talk to her, and she, being the understanding friend she was, had told me to go ahead and come over.

It was obvious that she and Mike had been about to sit down to dinner, because the table was set for two and yummy-smelling aromas drifted out to the living room from the kitchen. But she'd assured me it was just crockpot stew and could wait as long as necessary, and had made me sit down on the couch so I could tell her what was going on.

Not that there was a whole lot to tell. Someone had killed Jessica Rosenthal, but I had no idea who. Then again, someone as unpleasant as she'd appeared to be probably had plenty of people who wouldn't mind seeing her hastened along to the next plane of existence.

"Anyway," Deanne went on, echoing my own thoughts of a moment earlier, "I have a feeling the police are going to find plenty of people with a motive for murdering that woman. She was just awful."

Yes, she was, but I didn't voice that thought aloud. My grandmother had always taught me not to speak ill of the dead, no matter what my thoughts on the subject might be.

"If that's the case," I replied, "then why would one of her enemies follow her all the way to Las Vegas just to kill her?"

Deanne's shoulders lifted, and she sent a questioning glance at Mike. Looking a little startled at being asked for his opinion on the subject—he'd never met Jessica Rosenthal, and therefore probably felt he wasn't qualified to comment on her character—he said, "Maybe the murderer thought he'd be able to get away with committing the crime in a small town like Las Vegas instead of someplace like L.A. or New York. It's not as if we have a dedicated homicide division here or anything."

Well, that was true. The entire police department consisted of about thirty individuals, if you counted the women who worked in dispatch but who weren't actual sworn officers. There was a street crimes unit, but that group of deputies' duties encompassed pretty much everything you could think of, from busting vandals who thought it would be fun to paint graffiti on one of the town's historic buildings, to investigating tips on meth labs or finding out who was distributing the latest deadly version of fentanyl.

"Maybe the local police aren't so great at solving murders," Deanne said. "But Skye is. Why would the murderer commit a crime like this in a place with its very own psychic detective?"

I thought this particular view of the situation might be pushing it a little too far, partly because I definitely wasn't a detective or connected to the police department in any way, and partly because I didn't even think of myself as psychic. Yes, I had dreams that helped guide me, and my tea leaf readings could sometimes be prophetic, but it wasn't as though I could just close my eyes and visualize who the murderer in a particular case might be.

Except...could I? There was so much I didn't know about the powers that had come to me from my mother's family and which finally seemed to be waking up. Was it possible I could use that same magic to track down a murderer?

That scenario seemed way too easy. I shook my head, saying, "I don't think anyone outside Las Vegas even knows about my involvement in those two cases. Nothing in the news accounts connected me to the Perry Lockhart investigation at all, and Tom Gallegos' murder was more of a local thing. It was in the Albuquerque news for a while, but again, I wasn't mentioned in any of those reports."

"Oh," Deanne said, looking deflated now that I'd shot down her latest theory. "Well, maybe the murderer came after Jessica Rosenthal here because the place where she lives has a lot of security. Don't those Hollywood types have cameras everywhere and security guards and stuff?"

While I had to admit that Max's house in Bel-Air probably had that level of security—and his ranch here in Las Vegas was pretty heavily guarded, too, with cameras along the perimeter of the property and his guards, Lou and Al, keeping a much more personal kind of watch—I kind of doubted a mid-level producer of a cable reality show could afford that kind of setup.

But maybe Jessica was paranoid and spent a lot more of her salary on keeping herself safe than the average person would. I knew hardly anything about her, so I couldn't begin to guess.

"Some of them," I allowed, which was the only comment I felt qualified to make on the subject. "I think we'll just have to wait and hear what the police have to say."

Deanne didn't look too thrilled at that prospect, probably because, after the last two murders had been solved by a rank amateur like me and not anyone on the force, she didn't have a lot of faith in whatever theories Captain DeVargas or her lieutenants might put forward.

Which I supposed was fair, even if it really wasn't Marie DeVargas's fault that I'd gotten a jump on her when it came to investigating those previous crimes.

"And since we don't really know anything yet," Mike put in, "we might as well go eat. It's getting late."

Those words made me cast a guilty glance at the clock. Sure enough, the hour was inching toward eight, well past the time when Deanne and Mike would normally have sat down to dinner. They tended to eat early, just like I did, thanks to the way she and I had to be at the coffee shop so early in the morning.

Deanne looked as though she wanted to protest, but I chimed in before she could say anything. "Mike's right," I told her. "We're definitely not going to learn anything else tonight, so we should have dinner. You don't want it to spoil, do you?"

"You'd have to leave it in the crockpot an awfully long time before stew would spoil," she countered, but she didn't offer any additional arguments, only got up from the couch so she could head into the kitchen.

I followed, and helped her get some dinner rolls from the oven where they'd been warming. In the meantime, Mike busied himself with opening a bottle of wine, a sight that relieved me enormously. No, I didn't drink wine with dinner every night, but that evening, I knew I could use a glass...or maybe two.

And because he could tell I didn't want to talk about Jessica Rosenthal's death when we had so little to go on, he instead steered the conversation toward Max and the movie he was working on, asking me if I had any idea when he was going to be back in town.

"Not really," I responded, and helped myself to a bite of stew. It was a recipe I'd given Deanne a while back, and it had turned out just perfect. Not for the first time, I thought of what a good friend she was, how she always seemed to be there exactly when I needed her. Hearing about Jessica's murder had been a heck of a shock, and I hadn't relished the idea of having to go home afterward and eat leftovers while sitting alone in my big, empty house. "I mean, Max keeps saying it should only be a few more days, but then a couple of days go by, and he comes back and tells me the same thing all over again. It's not like he can go into a lot of details, but I get the impression they've been rewriting portions of the script as they go along."

"That's got to be rough," Deanne said, while Mike sent her a sly grin.

"I don't know," he told her. "I think I could

put up with a job going a little long if I was earning what he makes per movie."

In response, she gave him a withering look. "Money isn't everything."

"No," Mike said agreeably. "But it's a hell of a lot."

I just shook my head as he reached over to pour another half inch of wine into my glass. No, I wasn't planning on getting too tipsy, since I had to drive home, but at least I knew I didn't have to work the next day and therefore could indulge myself just the tiniest bit.

We chatted and ate and drank, and before I knew it, more than two hours had slipped by. My phone had stayed silent the entire time, which I told myself shouldn't be too much of a surprise. True, Justin had bowed out of our date—for obvious reasons—but it wasn't as though he owed me a blow-by-blow of what he'd learned at the police station. Sooner or later, I'd get the details through the grapevine...most likely from my deputy friend Kyle, since he was the person best suited to pass along any tidbits relating to a police investigation...but even that might have to wait until Monday morning. The coffee shop was closed until then, and it was a lot harder, and more obvious, to drop by my house for a chat than it was to go by Levitation Latte.

I said my goodbyes to Deanne and Mike and

thanked them for dinner, then headed home. Luckily, I'd left a light on in the living room and another one in the kitchen, so I wasn't coming back to a completely dark house. Even so, a little chill went down my spine as I let myself in and hurriedly glanced around.

Because even though Deanne and Mike's and my speculation had all centered around Jessica's murder being committed by someone who knew her, what if it had been a completely random act of violence? True, the last two murders had been committed for revenge and out of greed by people who had some kind of connection to the victims, but that didn't mean Jessica might not have been targeted because she apparently was just ripe for robbery. Justin had hurried off after giving me only the bare minimum about what had happened, so for all I knew, further investigation would show that her laptop and phone and any other valuables had been taken from the vacation rental.

I practically itched to learn more details, but it was after ten o'clock on a Friday night, and I definitely didn't know Justin well enough to be calling him at that hour, especially when this wasn't anything close to an emergency. No, I'd just have to wait and see what news trickled in over the next couple of days.

Or...was that really my only alternative? After all, I'd stood in the same room just the night before and let my magic lift me from the floor. Who knew what I might be able to do when it came to uncovering the true identity of the killer?

Only one way to find out, I supposed.

I set my purse down on the coffee table, then headed into the kitchen to get myself a glass of water. While I wasn't sure I could even count myself as actually tipsy, I knew that getting some fluids in me that weren't alcoholic had to be a good idea.

Glass of water in hand, I returned to the living room and sat down on the couch. I allowed myself a few swallows of water as I contemplated the best way to go about this. The last two times I'd gone about trying to solve a murder, I'd used my tea leaves and some hints from my dreams to guide me to the correct conclusion.

But that was before I'd realized my magic could do so much more than that. Maybe it still would have been a better idea to break out my tea leaves and see what they had to tell me, and yet I just wasn't in the mood. For one thing, the leaves that tended to give the best readings were of the caffeinated variety, and I was feeling edgy enough already without adding something into the mix that might interfere with my sleep.

Better to see what these new talents of mine might be able to do.

I drank a little more water and then closed my

eyes, figuring I could try to visualize the crime scene and see if that approach might guide me in the right direction. No, I'd never been to the vacation rental in question, but I'd seen the photos from its listing on the Airbnb website, and I figured that should be enough to give me a decent point of reference.

The house wasn't very big, but Lorraine, its owner, had done a great job of keeping it updated without losing its original turn-of-the-century charm. She'd chosen neutral hues of ivory and beige for the furniture, accented with cheerful turquoise and soft coral to give the decor a vaguely Southwest feel, although there was absolutely nothing kitschy about it.

I did my best to hold the image of the space in my mind, then thought, *Show me what happened in this room when Jessica Rosenthal was killed.*

And...nothing. Oh, the image stayed steadier than I'd thought it might—I didn't have much experience with meditating or anything like that, so it wasn't as if I had a lot of practice focusing on one scene to the exclusion of all others—but absolutely nothing changed about the image at all. I might as well have been looking at a photo on a website, when instead what I'd really hoped for was to have that static picture turn into a moving one.

An exasperated sigh escaped my lips, and I opened my eyes.

"Great," I muttered.

Then again, that had been my first try. I hadn't learned to ride a bicycle the first day, so why should this be any different?

You can do this, I told myself, but deep down, I wasn't so sure. Just because I could get up and fly around the room didn't mean that same magic could suddenly make me psychic.

But since giving up after the first attempt seemed pretty gutless to me, I went ahead and closed my eyes again. If nothing else, those swallows of water might help to dilute the wine I'd drunk at Mike and Deanne's place earlier this evening, and if I just waited long enough, that inner eye would finally decide to open and show me something useful.

Unfortunately, this second attempt wasn't any more successful than the first. I sat there for what felt like an eternity but was probably no more than five minutes at the most, and then opened my eyes again.

It sure looked like my protest to Deanne earlier that I wasn't really a psychic had only been the sad truth.

Annoyed, I drank some more water and weighed my options. I could keep trying tonight, but my head was starting to hurt and I had the sinking feeling that no matter how many times I made the attempt, I wouldn't accomplish anything more than giving myself a massive headache.

Besides, what was the real urgency here? True, no one liked the idea of a murderer running around town, but—my heebie-jeebies of a few minutes earlier notwithstanding—I really did believe that Jessica Rosenthal had been targeted on purpose, that this wasn't some random act of violence. If that turned out to be the case, I didn't see the harm in holding back and letting Chief DeVargas and the rest of the Las Vegas police department try to figure it out.

Also, tomorrow I'd be feeling a lot fresher mentally and could see what the tea leaves wanted to tell me.

You know, that sounded like a great idea.

I picked up my purse and the half-empty glass of water, and headed toward the kitchen. Just as I set the glass down on the countertop, figuring I'd leave it there and then rinse it out and reuse it in the morning, my phone rang from inside my purse.

Out of reflex, I glanced across the room at the clock on the microwave. Almost ten forty-five, which was weird. Nobody called me at that hour.

Had I left something behind at Deanne's? I didn't think so, but even if I had, she could have called me in the morning so I could drive over and get it whenever I had the chance. Nothing I might have inadvertently left at her house would have warranted a call this late.

But because I knew as well as anyone else that most late-night phone calls carried a certain urgency, I went ahead and got my phone out of my purse. I didn't recognize the number on the home screen, but the 212 area code got all my alarms pinging.

The only person I knew who had that area code was my mother.

"Alicia?" I said as soon as I swiped to accept the call and put my phone to my ear. "What is it?"

Her voice sounded resigned and maybe just the slightest bit amused.

"Can you come over to the police station?" she asked. "I just posted bail and need a ride home."

"'Bail'?" I repeated, not sure whether I'd heard her correctly. "For what?"

A faint chuckle came through the phone's speaker. "For Jessica Rosenthal's murder."

CHAPTER 8

Cloud of Suspicion

"Why in the world would Chief DeVargas think you killed Jessica Rosenthal?" I asked my mother.

We were back at the Hotel Castañeda, in a room that had been furnished with pretty antiques and archival photos of Las Vegas back in the early 1900s. When I'd picked her up at the police station, Alicia had told me she didn't want to talk right then and only wanted to go to her hotel. She didn't look quite as shaken as I'd expected, but I still hadn't argued.

No, I'd just driven her here, although we'd made a detour to a gas station so she could get herself a cup of coffee. I'd protested that we could swing by Levitation Latte and I'd make her some of the real stuff and not that nasty crap, but she'd told me she didn't want to make me go to all that trouble.

Now she sipped from the go-cup she'd bought and did her best to conceal a grimace as she swallowed the gas station coffee, which probably didn't taste much better than discarded motor oil from one of the station's oil changes.

"Because your police chief knows I had a beef with Ms. Rosenthal," Alicia said. For someone who'd just posted bail a half hour earlier, she appeared remarkably calm.

"Because of the way you stuck up for me?" I asked, trying my best to fit all the pieces together. "But no one else was even in the shop when that happened!"

Well, other than Deanne, but I knew my best friend would never rat out my mother, no matter what her personal feelings regarding the woman might be.

"True," Alicia replied. She drank some more coffee, and apparently was now used enough to the taste that she didn't even wince as it went down. "It sounds like Jessica headed back to where her team is working on the cowboy emporium and decided to air her grievances there. I suppose someone on her crew must have said something to the police."

"Isn't that hearsay?" I asked. Not that I pretended to know all the inner workings of the legal system, but I knew I'd heard that term thrown around on one of the legal shows my grandmother used to watch.

The smile Alicia sent me then wasn't exactly indulgent, but I got the definite feeling she thought I was being a bit naive. "This isn't a trial," she said. "All your police chief is looking for right now are any clues that might send her in the right direction. I'm a newcomer here, and one who doesn't have that great a reputation with the people in your town. And I did argue with Jessica. Chief DeVargas thinks I might have lashed out to compensate for abandoning you all those years ago."

That sounded like awfully twisted logic to me, but at the same time, I supposed I could see why the police chief might believe Alicia, desperate to prove herself to me, had decided to remove someone who was definitely a thorn in my side.

"But the judge still let you out on bail," I said slowly, and my mother gave a fatalistic shrug.

"Both he and the local attorney I was assigned probably realized Chief DeVargas didn't have enough evidence to hold me. This way, though, she can make sure to keep me around in case she doesn't come up with any more viable suspects."

For some reason, I felt almost heartened that Alicia wouldn't be heading out of Las Vegas any time soon. No, she hadn't mentioned a fixed time for her departure, but she also hadn't offered to give me any more lessons in magic, almost as though she believed that now she'd given me the key to unlock my gifts, she didn't really need to do anything more for me.

And while my feelings regarding her were still muddled at best, I had to believe having a little extra time around her must be a good thing...even if her reason for staying in town was that the conditions of her bail required her to do so.

But since I knew she had to have a life elsewhere, I asked, "Is that going to be a problem?"

She drank some more of her motor oil/coffee. "Do you mean, is anyone going to miss me?" A faint smile curved her lips, and she went on, "I have family in New York, but they know I come and go as I please, so it's not as if they're expecting me back any time soon. And while I have some obligations I can't neglect forever, they're nothing that can't wait until this mess is cleared up."

"Well, that's good," I said. "I mean, the whole thing stinks, but I'm glad it's not going to cause problems for you back home."

It felt a little weird to think how her home was most definitely not my home, and probably never would be. Not that I had any desire to live in New York City, but so far she hadn't said word one about me at least visiting there and getting to know that side of my family.

Did she think I was a hick, someone who

would only embarrass her if she took me to the East Coast with her?

I told myself not to borrow trouble and that we had plenty to worry about right here in Las Vegas. "Did Chief DeVargas say how long she thought all this would take?"

"No," Alicia responded, "and I really didn't expect her to. The investigation's just getting started, after all. But if this drags on longer than a week, I'll have to talk to my attorney again—he's not a criminal defense lawyer, so he told me to work with someone local for now—and see what he can do to make this go away. Honestly, I hadn't really planned to leave before then, anyway, and I told him that when he said he wanted to fly out right away to represent me."

Despite the circumstances, I couldn't help being a little cheered that she hadn't planned to leave in the immediate future. True, giving up a week to meet her daughter when she'd been out of my life almost thirty years wasn't exactly what you could call an equal balance sheet, but I figured I'd take what I could get.

And of course she had a lawyer on retainer. It seemed pretty obvious to me that she existed in a world as rarefied as Max's Hollywood circles, even if its particular flavor seemed to be completely different. "Well, it won't take that long," I announced confidently as a sudden thought took hold of me.

"You sound very sure of yourself," Alicia said, one eyebrow lifted in not-quite amusement.

"I am," I said. "Because I'm going to find the real killer and make sure you're exonerated."

Alicia hadn't shot me down, mostly because she knew I had some actual bona fides to back up my announcement that I was going to clear her name. But she also told me she was tired and wanted to go to bed, and I hadn't protested, if only because I knew I also needed to get my rest so I could attempt a tea-leaf reading the next day.

I found myself hoping I might have a true dream that night, something to provide an action-able clue as to who'd wrapped that phone charging cord around Jessica's neck, but no such luck. Instead, I had one of those stressful not-quite-nightmares where I was back at Levitation Latte trying to make coffee for what looked like an endless line of customers snaking out of the build-ing, only to open the supply cabinet and discover I was completely out of filters.

Sigh.

That dream left me annoyed and wanting anything except coffee the next morning, so I made myself a pot of tea. Not something I could use to read leaves with, because I was setting that activity aside for later in the morning, after I'd eaten and showered and was feeling a little more human.

No, this was a plain old pot of English Breakfast, accompanied by scrambled eggs and toast with plenty of butter and homemade apricot preserves. The meal helped brighten my outlook a little, as did the long, hot shower I took afterward before getting dressed and heading back downstairs.

I checked my phone as I went into the kitchen, but I hadn't missed any calls or messages. That was a little disappointing, if only to be expected. I doubted Deanne had heard much about the case yet, and Kyle was probably waiting for Monday morning when I was back at the shop and he could drop by to gossip without anyone thinking too much of it.

As for Justin, I could only imagine that he must have his hands pretty full at the moment. Would the team from *Fix My Town* pull up stakes following the tragedy and leave Las Vegas—even though that would mean leaving the Mackenzies and Pastor Phil and everyone else hanging—or would they keep going?

True, the movie Max had been working on when the director was murdered had been shut down permanently, but the two cases weren't at all similar. *Perdition Road* had been Perry Lockhart's baby, a film that would never have gone into production at all if it hadn't been for his coaxing the project along. This particular episode of *Fix My Town,* on the other hand, probably wouldn't materially suffer from Jessica Rosenthal's absence. The crew would mourn her loss—or maybe not, considering what a pain in the rear she'd seemed to be—but there shouldn't be anything to prevent them from wrapping up the episode without her.

If that proved to be the case, then Justin would probably be extra-busy for the next five weeks, since he'd have to cover Jessica's responsibilities in addition to his own. Maybe the cable network would send in a replacement producer to help out, or maybe not.

Either way, I didn't think I should expect to hear from him any time soon. Which was fine. He was cute, but I could only imagine that if I'd gone out with him more than once—and maybe even shared a kiss—I would have been assaulted by even more guilt than I already had by simply agreeing to the one dinner. It still felt like cheating to me, despite the troublesome fact that Max and I weren't a couple, and it was kind of hard to be unfaithful to someone who wasn't even your romantic partner.

As best I could, I pushed all those nagging thoughts away. Working with tea leaves required a calm and rested mind that was open to whatever the leaves might have to tell you, and roiling up my brain with thoughts of Max and might-have-beens with Justin Hale was exactly the opposite of what I needed to be doing right then.

I got out my favorite antique teacup, the one that had the perfectly sloped sides which worked the best for my forays into tasseography, and then went over to the stove and turned on the gas under the kettle, which I'd filled right after I was done with breakfast. It would take a few minutes for the water to boil, but that was all right. I needed that time to get my head clear.

At this time of year, the view of the backyard from my kitchen table wasn't exactly inspiring, since the lawn was yellow from frost and the flowerbeds looked as if I wouldn't be growing anything except mud there for the foreseeable future. But the branches of the cottonwoods and the oaks were graceful despite their current bare state, and I could let myself imagine what they would look like three months from now, with fat green buds on those leaves and the roses that my grandmother loved so much getting ready to provide me with a summer of gorgeous colors.

Was that a snowflake I just spied?

I tilted my head upward toward the gray skies outside the window—Friday had been clear, but more clouds had moved in overnight—and narrowed my eyes. Yes, that was definitely a fat white flake drifting down toward the garden path, followed by another, floating on a wind only they seemed to detect, because the air itself seemed still.

Good thing I hadn't planned on going anywhere today.

The snow we generally got in Las Vegas wasn't really heavy enough to keep you from driving to work or the store or whatever. Several times over the winter, we'd have a storm big enough to truly sock everything in, but I doubted that was going to happen today. No, this was just a quiet, gentle snowfall, enough to make everything pretty without actually sticking to the roads.

Watching the snow had an almost hypnotic effect on me, to the extent that I jumped a little when the teakettle began to whistle. I hurried over to the stove and turned off the gas, and then waited a minute for the boil to settle before I poured the hot water over the gunpowder green tea leaves I'd already placed in the cup.

Both hands wrapped around the teacup, I walked over to the table and sat back down. For a long moment, I was quiet, hands still holding the fragile porcelain, letting my mind focus on the question I needed to have answered.

Who killed Jessica Rosenthal?

Maybe that hadn't been the right way to ask the question—tea-leaf reading tended to focus on more abstract queries regarding "how" or "why," rather than providing an actual name—but it was too late now. Besides, even symbolic answers could be helpful in guiding me toward the truth.

I lifted the teacup to my lips and took a cautious sip. Yes, the liquid inside was hot, but not so hot that I had to worry about burning my tongue or lips. Still thinking about who would have had a reason to kill Jessica Rosenthal, I slowly drank the green tea until it was almost gone, and then placed the teacup's matching saucer over it and turned it upside down. The small amount of liquid that had been left behind drained into the saucer, giving me a proper canvas to work with.

Turning the cup right-side up again, I set the saucer aside and peered down into the cup. There were the usual bits of flotsam and jetsam stuck to the sides and the bottom, but one shape in particular caught my eye.

A heart.

This wasn't the first time I'd seen a heart in one of these readings, since hearts tended to be one of the most common shapes to present themselves in the debris left behind after the tea had been poured out. In fact, I'd spied one when I was performing a reading to discover who'd killed Perry Lockhart. At the time, I couldn't figure out why the heart had been there...until I realized much later that it was because Raylene Bryant's jealous husband had committed the murder in order to frame Max.

A twisted affair of the heart, but still, in the end it made sense.

So...had Jessica Rosenthal been killed by a jealous lover? Putting aside my dislike for the woman, I had to admit she was attractive enough in a brittle, high-strung kind of way. Not the sort of person I would have thought would inspire the kind of obsessive love that might lead to murder, but I'd be the first to admit I couldn't even pretend to always understand people's motivations.

If that was the case, then Deanne's theory about someone following Jessica to Las Vegas in order to kill her in a place where the murder investigation might not be up to big-city standards made some sense.

Or maybe the heart meant something else entirely. Maybe Jessica had been having an affair with someone, and that person's significant other was the killer.

Both possibilities seemed equally possible, if not entirely plausible.

Problem was, I just didn't know enough about the woman to make an educated guess.

Which meant I needed to do a little digging.

I got up from my chair, went to the kitchen sink, and then washed off the teacup and saucer before drying them with the handy dishcloth I always had hanging from a hook nearby. The porcelain was too fragile to go in the dishwasher, and in a way, I enjoyed this part of the ritual, felt like it put a period to my tea-leaf reading.

Now, though, I needed to do something very different.

All the bedrooms in the house were located upstairs, so I made my way to the second floor and headed into the one I'd turned into my office. It wasn't as though I spent a lot of time in there; when I wasn't at Levitation Latte, I tended to be downstairs in the kitchen...or in the living room when I wanted to put my feet up and read a book or watch some TV.

But I'd bought a cute little two-tone desk and some matching file cabinets, and hung a bulletin board where I could pin up pictures from magazines or anything else that caught my eye, and the room was just as "done" as my bedroom and the entire first floor. I had one bedroom left that was sort of a storeroom but which I kept meaning to turn into a guest room.

Not that I had a lot of guests coming to visit— my extended family lived mostly in Texas and had only come back to Las Vegas for my grandmother's funeral and then headed straight home and stayed there—but you never knew.

Anyway, my laptop waited for me on the desk, so I opened it up and entered my password, then went to IMDB to see what I could find on Jessica Rosenthal.

It definitely looked as though she'd been working in the industry pretty much ever since she graduated from film school at USC. She was a native of Southern California and had started out as a production assistant, then quietly moved her way up the ladder until she began getting executive producer credits, culminating with her job on *Fix My Town.*

I found that piece of information somewhat interesting, mainly because Justin had made it sound as though they were co-producers. Well, maybe he was an executive producer as well but had decided to leave out the "executive" part so he wouldn't sound too puffed up about his position.

A quick search of his name showed a similar career trajectory, except he was listed as a regular producer on *Fix My Town,* not one of the executive variety. An oversight on his part?

Something to ponder later. For now, while her IMDB credits had provided a little more information about Jessica Rosenthal's professional career, it hadn't told me anything about her personal life beyond mentioning where she'd gotten her degree.

Time to do a little more poking around.

A Google search turned up scores of Jessica Rosenthals, but when I added "Fix My Town" to the search parameters, it narrowed the results so I could get more directed information, including a link to her website. It didn't contain much beyond a recitation of her major producing credits, though, which I supposed made sense. The website was intended to provide information about her professional career, not tell the entire world what was going on in her personal life.

However, she also had a Wikipedia page, although I got the impression it had been posted by someone else and not the woman herself. But at least it mentioned that she was thirty-seven years old and that she'd been divorced for more than five years and didn't have any children, a factoid which seemed to tell me at least we weren't dealing with a jealous husband here.

Jealous boyfriend or girlfriend?

Maybe. Nothing I'd read so far seemed to indicate Jessica Rosenthal had much of a personal life, which made sense when you looked at her producing credits and realized she'd pretty much worked all those projects back to back and therefore wouldn't have had time for something as frivolous as dating.

But even though the Wikipedia article had given me a bit more information, it still hadn't provided me with enough data to form a clear picture of the woman.

And, unlike some other tea-leaf readings I'd performed—like the one I'd done to try to find out who had killed Tom Gallegos, a reading that had shown me a clover and a shovel, both clues that eventually led me right to his murderous brother—this current one had shown me only a heart and nothing else, so I didn't even have an additional symbolic guide to find out why the heart was so important in Jessica's case.

Using my powers hadn't helped a bit, either.

I let out a sigh and sat back in my office chair, twirling one strand of hair idly as I stared at the screen of my MacBook Air. Jessica's face gazed back at me from her IMDB page, looking a lot friendlier than she ever had in my encounters with her. The image was clearly a professional head shot she'd had done for her website, and she looked polished and breezy and as if she was exactly the right person to choose for your next producing job.

Although I definitely couldn't say I'd liked her, she also hadn't deserved to end up strangled on the floor of a rented house.

"Who killed you?" I said aloud, but of course her image didn't answer, only continued to stare back at me from the computer screen.

Clearly, I was going to have to look somewhere else for answers.

CHAPTER 9

Dream a Little Dream

The rest of the day was quiet enough. I texted Alicia and asked if she wanted to come over for dinner, but she demurred, saying she planned to get room service and lie low for now.

I'd love to take you out for dinner while I'm here, she wrote back. *But considering everything that's going on, I think it's better to maintain a low profile. I'll probably take a drive tomorrow if the weather clears up.*

Which looked iffy at the moment. The snow had come and gone all day, sometimes hard enough that a little bit would begin to accumulate in the garden and along the top of the fence that enclosed the yard, at other times letting up enough that blue sky peeked through every once in a while. Luckily, the roads still looked pretty clear, so I guessed Alicia shouldn't have too much trouble getting around as long as she didn't try to drive up into the mountains. Because of the cloud cover, I couldn't see much of them, but I had to believe it was snowing pretty hard up there.

To be honest, I knew I should have headed out to the store to stock up on a few things. However, this kind of weather only made me want to cocoon at home, so I gave in to the urge, puttering around the kitchen as I whipped up some chicken corn chowder for dinner, tidying up here and there before I ended my day with a bowl of soup in front of the TV while I watched a couple of past episodes of *Fix My Town*. Why I'd settled there, when I doubted those shows would provide any useful evidence, I didn't know for sure. I suppose I'd hoped I'd spy a small clue, something that would help me figure out why someone had seen the need to murder Jessica Rosenthal while she worked on the show's new season.

But I didn't see a darn thing. In some of the shots, you could catch a glimpse of the production team as they interacted with the show's hosts, but Jessica never appeared in any of those clips. I thought I heard Justin off camera once or twice, which didn't tell me much except that he'd obviously been there doing his job.

However, seeing the show's hosts—a contractor named Eddie Trask and interior designer Maggie McCall—got me wondering. I hadn't seen anything of them since the *Fix My Town* team had arrived in Las Vegas, but that didn't seem too strange. After all, they'd be on the scene of projects that were already in process, and since Jessica had still been in the process of negotiating with me as to whether Levitation Latte was even going to appear in this particular episode, there wouldn't have been any reason for them to be hanging around the shop.

Still, it couldn't hurt to see if I could track them down and chat them up. Even if the powers-that-be ultimately decided to go on with the show after Jessica's Rosenthal's death, the production team was probably going to be idle for a few days until the honchos at the cable network decided how they should proceed.

And actually, it wasn't as though I'd have to do much detective work to figure out where the crew actually was, since it sounded as though the entire *Fix My Town* team—other than Justin and Jessica —was staying at the Plaza Hotel. With nothing much else to occupy their time until they could start shooting again, I had to believe they were probably wandering around downtown, trying to decide what to do with themselves.

Which meant I needed to figure out what I might do tomorrow that would send me across their paths. Too bad the coffee shop wasn't open, but I'd already tried the ploy of opening Levitation

Latte when it wasn't normal business hours back when Perry Lockhart was killed. The scheme had worked well enough, and yet I had a feeling if I tried that maneuver again, people would know I was only doing so in order to dig up information about Jessica Rosenthal's murder.

Well, I'd come up with something. In the meantime, though, it was time to go to bed.

I headed upstairs and performed my usual nightly ritual of washing up, brushing and flossing, and applying moisturizer, then turned off the lights and climbed under the covers. In the winter, I kept a big fluffy down comforter on the bed, since the house tended to be drafty despite all the improvements I'd made a few years earlier.

And even though it hadn't worked so well when I'd tried to summon a psychic flash about the killer, I thought I might as well make the attempt again, only this time to have those powers send me one of my infrequent prophetic dreams. I closed my eyes and didn't exactly articulate the request, only sent out the intention that it would be really, really nice if I could actually dream about something useful tonight.

I was one of those lucky people who tended to fall asleep easily, so it didn't take long before I drifted into welcome darkness. For a while, my dreams were jumbles of ordinary enough things, like wandering through the house and looking for a feather duster —I didn't actually own one, since I wiped down all my furniture with microfiber cloths—or standing behind the counter at Levitation Latte and trying to grind the beans by crushing them in my hands.

Later that night, though, I came swimming back up into REM sleep, and I saw Jessica Rosenthal standing in a room that looked as though it might have been her office back in Los Angeles, a modern space with glass and stainless steel furniture and pale gray paint on the walls. She looked different here, wearing a sleek black suit and cream silk blouse, although her dark blonde hair was still pulled back into its ubiquitous ponytail.

Her voice, however, was the same, sounding almost as annoyed as she had when she'd tried to cajole me into letting the *Fix My Town* team remodel the coffee shop.

"You know that's impossible," she snapped. "I'm not going to stick my neck out when it's obvious you're not ready for the job."

Who was she talking to? In my dream, she stood turned halfway away from me, speaking to someone who was maddeningly out of eyeshot. Worse, when they made some sort of response, their voice was jumbled and distorted, sounding like one of the adults in an old *Peanuts* cartoon.

About the only thing I could tell was that the

sound felt male to me, just slightly deeper than a woman's voice would be.

Well, that narrowed things down...not.

"Anyway," she went on, "I've got things to do. Prove yourself on this next project, and maybe we can talk. Just don't get caught with your pants down, or I'll make sure you never work in this town again."

The dream faded then, and I blinked awake, allowing myself a quick glance at the clock on the nightstand—it was a little after 4 a.m.—before I rolled over and stared up at the ceiling. Because the curtains at the windows weren't light-blocking, I could see the faintest traces of bare branches outlined against the plaster, moving with the wind.

I shivered, even though I was definitely warm enough under my down comforter.

Who had Jessica been talking to?

Someone who'd apparently been involved in some sort of indiscretion, even though the snippet of conversation hadn't included enough detail to give me much context. And why had the man's voice been distorted that way?

But dreams were weird, even ones that eventually turned out to be true. This particular dream definitely felt as though it was real—the details about Jessica's office and even the clothes she'd been wearing felt far too real, too specific. I had to believe I'd been given a glimpse of a scene that had taken place sometime in the past, although exactly when, I didn't know.

Had there been a calendar on her desk or on the wall, or anything on the computer's screen that would give me some context?

I frowned, doing my best to recall every single item I'd glimpsed in that office, but it didn't seem to help much. As far as I could tell, there weren't any calendars anywhere to be found, and although her laptop had been open on the desk, it had been angled away toward the window, making it impossible to see anything.

"Why send me a dream if it isn't going to have anything useful in it?" I grumped aloud. Sometimes I liked to talk to myself, as though hearing my own voice could provide some reassurance.

Right then, however, I was feeling anything but reassured. Without seeing who Jessica was talking to, I had no way of knowing why that particular conversation had been so important.

Like the heart I'd seen in my teacup the day before, its meaning wouldn't be revealed until after I'd finally stumbled my way through the puzzle.

Frowning, I closed my eyes and pulled the covers a little farther up my neck, hoping that maybe I'd be visited by a second true dream that night, one which would provide the details I was looking for.

Unfortunately, I didn't dream at all after I went back so sleep. All right, I probably did have some dreams, but I didn't remember any of them, which was kind of the same thing.

I was feeling cranky as I brewed that morning's coffee and brooded over what to do next. It probably didn't help that the snow had thickened overnight, leaving about three inches on the ground before the storm finally decided to move on. The sun was out, and the backyard looked like a picture on a holiday card, but that didn't cheer me up much. I would have loved to see a scene like that right around Christmas. In early February, it only served to remind me that we probably had at least six weeks more of winter before the weather finally began to warm up.

Coffee in hand, I wandered out to the living room so I could peek past the curtains and see what the streets were like. To my relief, they looked clear despite the snow that coated the trees and my neighbors' yards, so I didn't see any reason why I couldn't head downtown later and find out if there was any information I could dig up from the *Fix My Town* crew.

Including whether any of them knew anything about that supposed "indiscretion" Jessica had been talking about in my dream. That was a topic

I'd have to approach with some delicacy, but because it was the only real clue I had to work with at the moment, I couldn't exactly avoid it.

If it hadn't been a Sunday, I might have texted Deanne to see if she wanted to come with me and play Watson to my admittedly clumsy Sherlock Holmes. But she and Mike were both active in their church, and always stayed after services for the communal potluck they held for lunch. Most of the time, she didn't get home until well after one o'clock, and then the two of them usually needed to do whatever chores they hadn't been able to get to during the week.

No, I'd definitely have to take on this fact-finding mission solo.

It was a little after eleven when I left the house, mostly because I wanted to make sure my hair was completely dry after I washed it so I wouldn't be wandering around in thirty-degree weather with wet roots. Although I resorted to a blow dryer and a curling iron when I had to, on the weekends I liked to let my hair go natural in order to give it a break.

The snow had stopped, however, and the skies overhead were mostly blue. I still drove carefully, though, since the streets, while not exactly icy, were slick enough that a hard stop would have sent me spinning.

Not that there were really that many cars on

the roads, though. I got the impression that if people didn't have a reason to go out, then they planned to stay safely at home.

However, I didn't think the weather would have much effect on the *Fix My Town* people, since they were all staying at the Plaza Hotel and therefore could walk pretty much anywhere downtown they wanted to go.

Unless, of course, they'd gotten the word from the higher-ups at the cable network that work was being stopped on this particular episode and they all could go home.

I hadn't noticed unusual amounts of traffic heading out of town, though, nothing like the caravan of trucks and work vans Deanne had reported seeing when everyone arrived in Las Vegas on Thursday morning. It was a little hard to believe that only three days had passed since then—with all the upheaval in my own life, thanks to Alicia Petrucci appearing out of nowhere, it felt as though it had to have been at least three weeks.

There was more foot traffic around the plaza than I'd been expecting, telling me that people wanted to get out and breathe in some fresh air, even if the air in question hovered right around the freezing mark. In fact, one of those people raised a hand to wave at me, and I realized the person was none other than Justin Hale.

I hurried over to him, glad of my rubber-soled boots on the icy sidewalk.

"Hey," he said, as soon as I got close enough. "Sorry I've been out of touch."

"It's fine," I reassured him. "You've kind of had a lot going on."

Justin grimaced. He was wearing a puffer coat and a pine green knitted cap that squashed his light brown hair beneath it, and I noted the dark stubble that covered his chin and cheeks. It definitely looked to me as though he hadn't shaved since Friday.

"Still," he said, then paused and looked over at the elaborate façade of the Plaza Hotel, only a few yards away. "It's freezing out here. Want to go inside and have a cup of coffee or something?"

That had been my basic plan, although I had to admit it was a stroke of luck that Justin was the first person I'd encountered here. Now I wouldn't have to worry about trying to strike up a conversation with a stranger, the kind of interaction that generally made me want to break out in hives.

"Or something," I agreed. "I already had coffee this morning, but some hot chocolate would be great."

A grin, and he gestured for me to follow him across the street and inside the building. Because it was a little late for breakfast and too early for lunch, we were able to get a table inside the hotel's café right away, with the bonus of window seats so we had a good view of the park.

We placed our orders right away, and soon enough, I had a cup of hot chocolate topped with whipped cream in front of me, while Justin opted for a cappuccino liberally sprinkled with cinnamon. The coffee in the Plaza wasn't as good as mine, of course, but it was decent enough, and I had to admit their hot chocolate was heavenly.

After we'd both taken our first sips, I asked, "How're you holding up?"

His shoulders lifted. He'd taken off the puffer coat as we sat down, showing the green and blue plaid flannel shirt he wore underneath. Combined with the stubble on his chin, the ensemble made him look like a yuppie who'd decided to spend a weekend in the woods and wasn't sure whether he really liked it or not.

"Okay," he said, after sipping some more of his cappuccino. "I mean, it's been crazy, as you can imagine. Because we were so early in the process here, some of the higher-ups at the channel wanted to pull the plug on the whole thing. I think I've talked them down, though."

Well, that was something. Just because I hadn't wanted Jessica Rosenthal and her team to tear apart Levitation Latte didn't mean the rest of the people in town who were genuinely excited about their makeovers should have to miss out.

"So, the show is still going on?"

Justin nodded. "Looks that way. We take Sunday off regardless of what else might be happening, which is why we're all sort of out and about today. The police are still poking around the Airbnb, so I had to move my stuff to the hotel. Luckily, a room opened up late Friday, or I would've been sleeping on a cot in one of the other crew members' rooms."

That probably wouldn't have been very comfortable. I had to admit I was a little surprised that the police were taking so long with the crime scene, but maybe they wanted to make sure no one could accuse them of not being thorough. And because Jessica Rosenthal's murder had taken place at an Airbnb and not a private residence, it was possible they didn't feel the same sense of urgency about allowing the residents back home.

"Yes, that was lucky," I agreed, then paused so I could sip some more hot chocolate and decide on the best way to ask the question that had been floating around in my mind. A direct approach was probably best, especially since I didn't see the need to beat around the bush. "Do you know if Jessica was involved with anyone, maybe in a situation where someone would be jealous enough to murder her?"

For a second, Justin just stared back at me, brow knotted in what might have been consternation...or maybe plain old confusion. "What makes you ask that?"

Now it was my turn to pause. Obviously, I hadn't said anything to him about my tea-leaf reading hobby, since our date had ended before it even got started, and it wasn't exactly the sort of thing that came up in casual conversation.

"Well...." I began, then took a breath. Might as well go for it. "I did a tea-leaf reading about her death, and the only real clue that came up indicated it was a crime of passion, or at least that something about a love life was involved."

Justin gave an uneasy laugh. "You're joking, right?"

"No," I replied, telling myself not to be offended. After all, tasseography was kind of out there, even among people who wouldn't have a second thought about using Tarot cards or collecting crystals. "It's something I've been doing for a while, and it's usually pretty accurate. But my reading about Jessica turned up a heart shape in my cup, which always means something related to love. That's why I was wondering if maybe she was cheating on someone, or cheating with someone. Anything that might have made the murderer strike at her in a rage."

"Nothing I know of," Justin said. His expression told me he was still pretty skeptical about the whole tea-leaf thing but was willing to let it go for now. "She's been divorced for years, and, as far as I know, she wasn't seeing anyone. Work was pretty much her whole life."

A conclusion I'd already begun to draw after reading the brief biographical information I'd found on IMDB and Wikipedia. Well, sometimes the tea leaves goofed up, or I just hadn't interpreted them correctly. Maybe what I'd thought was a heart was really a skull, which made more sense when you got right down to it.

"Oh," I said. Not the most brilliant of responses, but I didn't know quite where else to go from here if love wasn't a motive in the crime somehow. "Have the police said anything?"

"Not much," Justin responded. I could tell he wasn't thrilled that they didn't have any definitive answers yet, because a small, worried crease appeared between his eyebrows as he pondered the problem. But then he lifted his cappuccino and drank from the cup before adding, "The medical examiner thinks she died sometime around seven, but that's about it."

Right when I was meeting Justin at the Hotel Castañeda. It was hard to think about the woman dying violently just as I was looking forward to a date with him, but obviously, neither one of us could have had any idea what was happening less than a mile from our meeting place.

"So, the girl who found her must have gotten there right after it happened," I murmured.

"Cecily?" Justin said, then went on before I could respond, "Yeah, she was pretty shaken up, poor kid. The police questioned her for a long time, but she didn't see anyone when she drove up to the house, so it sounds like she must have just missed the murderer."

"Scary."

Another nod. "She was definitely freaked, thinking that if she'd been just a few minutes earlier coming over to the house with those forms, she might've been a victim, too. Right now, it sounds like the cops think it must have been a robbery gone wrong—Jessica's laptop was stolen, and her credit cards were missing. It doesn't sound as if there were any fraudulent charges on the cards, though, so I guess the thief thought better of using them. The laptop, though—it was a brand-new MacBook Pro with all the bells and whistles, and probably could have gotten the thief at least a couple grand on the street."

This was all news to me. But then, I hadn't had a chance to talk to Kyle yet, or I probably would have known the local P.D. was looking at the crime as possibly a robbery gone wrong. However, I had to believe it was just one theory they were entertaining, or they surely would have dropped the charges against my mother.

And yet....

Something about the situation didn't feel right to me. I couldn't really put my finger on it, except —despite wondering if the heart really had been a skull after all—I somehow knew in my gut that this wasn't a simple crime of opportunity and nothing more. For one thing, if Jessica really had startled an intruder, why had he strangled her with a phone cord? That seemed an oddly personal murder weapon to me, when even hitting her over the head with a lamp or some other blunt object sounded more like the sort of thing a home invader would do if he'd decided not to use a gun, for whatever reason.

But I'd be the first to admit that I wasn't exactly an expert on the criminal mind, so maybe the guy had grabbed the phone charging cord because it had been the first thing he saw.

"Did she have 'Find My Mac' installed on her computer?" I asked next. Not that I was an expert, but because I'd bought my own laptop only a year earlier, I knew the program existed, and I had it running on my little MacBook Air. No, it hadn't been as expensive as Jessica's Pro, but that didn't mean I wanted someone to steal it.

"I don't know," Justin said. "But I have to assume she didn't, or the police would've tracked it down by now, right?"

I supposed so. That is, she would've had to

have the same app installed on her phone or tablet, or there wouldn't have been any way to track down the stolen laptop. Or maybe the police could've gone straight to Apple to see if they could ping the computer and figure out where it had been taken.

Either way, it didn't look as though they'd found it, which meant she either didn't have the program installed, or it had been turned off.

"Probably," I said. Right then, I was feeling a little deflated about the whole thing, probably because I'd thought for sure the heart I'd seen in the teacup was a solid lead.

Luckily, though, it wasn't the only lead I had.

"Any professional enemies?" I asked next, and once again, Justin's brow furrowed.

"What do you mean?"

"Just...people she might have crossed while she was making her way up the ladder," I said. "I know I'm not an expert or anything, but the entertainment business can be kind of cutthroat, can't it?"

That question earned me an outright laugh. Justin picked up his cup of cappuccino, commenting, "I've seen people pull some dirty tricks, if that's what you mean. But I've never heard of anyone resorting to murder just because someone else got ahead of them."

No, I'd never heard of that, either, but then again, it wasn't as if I spent my days following what was going on in the entertainment world.

Well, beyond spending a little too much time tracking all of Max Sullivan's various movie projects.

And even though I'd told Justin about the way I read tea leaves, something was warning me not to mention that I also had prophetic dreams from time to time. Tasseography might be a kind of wacky hobby, but confessing I had dreams which came true?

That would send me right over into crackpot territory.

"Any reason why you would ask that?" he inquired, head tilting slightly to one side.

"No," I said hastily, and reached for my cup of hot chocolate. "I'm just kind of grasping at straws, I guess. Probably a waste of time, since it sounds like this was a robbery gone wrong and nothing more." I sipped some chocolate, licked the whipped cream from my upper lip, and added, "So...what now? Back to work tomorrow?'

Justin leaned against his seat, clearly relieved by the change of subject. "That's the plan. Luckily, it looks like there won't be any more snow until the end of the week at least, so we should be able to get a lot done." A pause, and he added, his tone sly, "Although we're still trying to figure out what to do with all that flooring Jessica ordered for your shop."

That reminder made my shoulders tense all

over again, even if it sounded as though he was teasing me more than anything else. "I'm really sorry about that—" I began, but Justin lifted a hand, cutting off my completely unnecessary apology.

"Don't be," he said. "It's her own fault for thinking she could bully you into changing your coffee shop. It's perfect the way it is, so I'm glad you fought back."

"You really think so?" I asked, knowing I blushed a little as I asked the question. Well, with any luck, he'd just think I was flushed from the temperature difference between the cold, snowy day outside and the café where we sat. To compensate for the weather, they had the thermostat turned up pretty high, and it was almost uncomfortably warm inside.

"Yes," he replied without a single bit of hesitation. "So much of what we do ends up looking way too same-y. It's like all the designers think there's just one type of interior decorating right now, and they try to make everything fit in that mold."

"Oh, they're not all like that," I told him, because that was only the truth. I'd watched enough home design and remodeling shows to know that, while there were definite trends that seemed to dominate to the exclusion of everything else, there were also designers who really seemed to take their clients' personal tastes and needs into consideration before they started ripping everything apart.

He shrugged. "Maybe not all. But a lot."

I could tell he was feeling more relaxed now, maybe because we were talking about more neutral topics like the show itself or design in general. Although he was doing his best to hide it, I got the feeling that Jessica's death had upset him more than he wanted to reveal, which made total sense. There didn't seem to have been anything intimate between the two of them, but the IMDB credits I'd looked up had shown that they'd been working together for the past three years, so they must have shared a personal connection forged by all those grueling production schedules and late nights.

But even though I was glad we'd met up, saving me from having to question other members of the crew about Jessica Rosenthal, I couldn't help feeling that our conversation hadn't given me very much additional information. True, Justin had pretty much shot down the idea that anyone would murder a colleague just to get ahead, but at the same time, I had to believe that dream of mine had been trying to tell me something, even if I couldn't quite figure out what it was.

The conversation drifted to the plans the designers had for the former cowboy emporium— where it sounded as though the *Fix My Town* team had already roughed in the plumbing and gas lines for a new kitchen—to the movie theater and a sign to be erected at the town's southern edge by Ben Fredricks, who was a noted local metal sculptor. All in all, it definitely sounded as though Las Vegas would be a lot more than a wide spot in the road by the time they were done, and even though Jessica Rosenthal's plans for Levitation Latte would never pan out, the town would still have enough updates that it would be sure to draw more travelers than it ever had before.

After we finished our coffee and hot chocolate, Justin excused himself, saying he needed to go over Jessica's notes for tomorrow's shoot. I didn't bother to protest, or try to draw out our meeting, since I knew he'd probably be doing the work of two until this particular project was wrapped up.

No, I headed for home, feeling vaguely dissatisfied. As far as I could tell, he'd been nothing but truthful with me, but I still had the nagging sensation there was something I'd overlooked, something that should have pushed me in the direction of whoever had killed Jessica Rosenthal.

As much as I picked at it with my mind, though, I couldn't think of anything that might be missing. From what I'd heard so far, it seemed clear enough to me that her death had been purely accidental, an unfortunate side effect of a robbery gone wrong.

So why did it feel so personal? Was it just that

odd detail of the phone charging cord being used as the murder weapon and nothing else?

I wanted to say that was the reason for my current unease, but my gut was telling me something entirely different. Exactly what, I didn't know. The only thing I did know was that when I got into this state, I needed to let it ride until something a lot more concrete presented itself.

A few flurries of snow fell as I drove home, certainly not enough to hinder my drive in any way. For some reason, I found myself thinking of Sunset Ridge, the ranch Max had bought a few months back. It was probably getting a little more snow than we were here in the heart of Las Vegas, if for no other reason than it sat on a promontory at least five or six hundred feet higher than the town, and so was prone to slightly more extreme weather.

I hadn't heard from him today, which I tried to reassure myself was no big deal. He was on set, and so had odd hours. Expecting him to drop everything so he could email me on a regular basis simply wasn't logical. He reached out when he had time, and I knew I should be happy for even that much, considering how busy he was.

All the same, I felt oddly let down as I entered the house. Maybe it was only that I didn't have any real plans, nothing I absolutely had to get done that day, but I didn't know what I should do with myself until it was time to go back to Levitation

Latte the next morning. Pretty sad that I was twenty-nine and had the social life of a resident in a retirement home, but there it was.

Come to think of it, most residents in retirement communities had more to do with their free time than I did, if you counted bingo nights and art classes and shuffleboard and Sadie Hawkins dances.

And I really, really hated that so far I hadn't come up with a single piece of substantial evidence to prove there was absolutely no way Alicia Petrucci could have murdered Jessica Rosenthal. I knew she hadn't done it, but going to Chief DeVargas with my gut feelings wasn't going to get me very far.

As usual when I felt frustrated, I retreated into the kitchen to bake. Not muffins and croissants, because I made enough of those particular pastries during the week to last me a lifetime, but snicker-doodles and chocolate chunk cookies. There was no way in the world I'd be able to eat them all on my own, of course, but I'd keep some to nibble on here at home, and then drop off plates of the remaining sweets at the local police and fire stations. It seemed like the least I could do to thank them for their service.

At a little past four, my phone pinged, and I wiped off my floury hands and picked it up so I could look down at the screen.

The text message was from Alicia.

Are you free tonight? I thought I could pick up some tacos from The Skillet and bring them over. There are still some things I want to discuss with you about your magic, but I don't want to make you cook for me again.

I almost wrote back that I didn't mind cooking, but then I stopped myself. It seemed clear enough that Alicia wanted to return the favor by providing the food this time, so I knew I shouldn't push back on her offer.

Sounds great. What time?

Six-thirty?

That works.

See you then.

And with that quick exchange, it looked as though I had my evening plans taken care of. Yes, six-thirty was a few hours from now, but I'd take that time to see that everything in the kitchen was properly tidied up, and to make sure the cookies I'd just baked were carefully stored in some Tupperware containers of mine, just waiting to be taken over to their respective police and fire stations the next morning when I could tear myself away from the coffee shop for a few minutes.

Alicia rang the doorbell at about a minute past six-thirty. By that hour, the intermittent snow had stopped, so even though it was still bitterly cold outside, the roads were clear, if maybe a bit icy.

However, she seemed to have made it to the house without incident, because she was right on time, holding a bag of takeout from The Skillet in one hand.

"Come in," I told her, then stepped out of the way so she could enter the living room. As soon as she was safely inside, I shut the door behind her. I knew the staff at the restaurant would have done their best to make sure our dinner was carefully wrapped up, but when it was already pushing the mid-twenties outside, food could get cold fast no matter how much you tried to swaddle it in layers of tinfoil. "The table's already set."

She followed me into the dining room, where our place settings waited for us, along with a pitcher of water. No wine, though, because she'd made it sound as if this dinner was going to be focused on talking about magic, and past experience had shown me it was a good idea not to mix the two.

A few minutes were spent divvying up the tacos she'd brought—beef barbacoa and carnitas and grilled chicken—and then I said, "Did you have a nice drive today?"

Alicia looked at me, expression halfway startled, and she replied, "Oh, I decided not to go out, since the weather was so iffy. I spent most of the day reading and relaxing."

"You could have come over sooner," I said, hoping my voice didn't sound too accusing.

"I suppose I probably could have," she responded, expression amused. "But I didn't want to impose. Anyway, I'd sort of forgotten how nice it feels to simply put my feet up and not have to do much of anything."

Because I'd had days like that of my own—few and far between, but still—I couldn't really argue with her statement. Instead, I poured some water from the pitcher into her glass and then into mine, and said, "So, what was it that you wanted to talk to me about?"

Her dark eyes glinted a little. "Oh, a lot of things. But I suppose I'm just a little surprised that you didn't have many more questions for me."

Actually, I had tons of them, so many that I didn't quite know which to ask first, which might have been the reason for my current mental gridlock on the subject. However, I figured I might as well start with the one that had been pricking at the back of my mind while I was working on baking all those cookies earlier in the day.

"I had a dream last night," I said. "One I think was a true one, although sometimes it's hard to be sure. But it didn't feel any different from any other 'true' dream I'd ever had."

Alicia reached for her glass of water and took a sip. "Why were you expecting it to be different?"

Good question, although this time I at least had a ready answer.

"Because I'd focused on tapping into my new powers, asking them to give me a true dream. I suppose I just thought if I was bringing those talents to bear, then I'd have a dream that was even more vivid and clear-cut than I was used to."

Was that a very small hint of a smile at the corner of her mouth? If so, she suppressed it quickly enough that I wasn't sure whether I'd just imagined it.

However, her tone was serious enough as she responded, "I think it's because the gifts of prophetic dreams and reading tea leaves come from your O'Malley side. The powers that are growing stronger in you right now are from the Petrucci side of the family. Our talents are more...physical, I suppose. We can affect the world around us or ourselves, but the world of dreams, of visions and anything that hasn't happened yet—all those are from your O'Malley great-grandmother, the one who had the Sight. They don't cross over. They just happened to combine in you."

Well, they "happened" to combine because Alicia had made sure to hook up with someone who carried those gifts in his blood, even if they hadn't manifested in him. I still didn't quite know what to do about this magical soup that ran in my veins, but I had to hope I'd get used to it someday.

"So, trying to force it doesn't work," I said, and she inclined her head the smallest bit before reaching for a barbacoa taco.

"No. You can work on your Petrucci magic—fine-tune it, see what the limits of your powers actually are—but with the O'Malley gifts, all you can really do is open yourself up to them and see where they guide you."

In other words, pretty much nothing on that front had changed. I tried to push back at the disappointment that rose in me at the thought, telling myself I'd been doing just fine before I started flying through the house, and I'd continued to do fine.

Besides, how could I force something that was as unpredictable and intangible as a dream? No, I really needed to learn to be Zen about those particular gifts.

Maybe instead of questioning Alicia, I should be teaching myself how to meditate.

The doorbell rang then, and she shot me a startled look.

"Were you expecting someone?"

"No," I said, even as I lifted the napkin from my lap and rose from my chair. After the events of the past few days, I wasn't quite sure what to expect. Chief DeVargas, with new information about Jessica Rosenthal's murder, coming to put my mother behind bars?

Even as the thought passed through my head, I did my best to dismiss it. There was no way in the world the police chief could even know Alicia was over at my house tonight.

Still, it seemed way too cold for random Girl Scouts to be knocking on my door and trying to sell me Samoas, and besides, it was the wrong time of year for that sort of thing.

My heart was beating faster than usual as I went to the door and opened it. Standing on the porch was Max Sullivan, his brilliant smile like a memory of warm summer days.

"Hey," he said. "Miss me?"

CHAPTER 10

Enter the Lion

For a second, I could only stare up at Max, wondering whether all the strain of the past few days had been too much and I'd suddenly started hallucinating.

But no, that really was my friend standing there on the doorstep, looking way more tanned and relaxed than the wintry landscape just beyond him would normally have warranted.

Then I found my voice saying, "Wow—this is a nice surprise. Come on in."

And I stepped aside, thinking he had a much bigger surprise waiting for him inside the house than he was probably expecting. At once, his gaze moved to the woman who sat at the dining room table, and one eyebrow lifted in question.

"Max, this is my mother, Alicia Petrucci," I said. "Alicia, this is Max Sullivan, a friend of mine."

At that introduction, Max looked absolutely flabbergasted, although Alicia didn't appear quite so astonished. Considering I'd already picked up several clues that she'd been paying a bit more attention to my life than I'd previously thought, this didn't surprise me as much as it once might have. She must have known that Max Sullivan had grown up right next door to me, and she probably also knew that the two of us had renewed our friendship after he came back to Las Vegas to shoot *Perdition Row* and had decided to buy the ranch and settle here, if only part-time.

But she smiled as she stood and extended a hand saying, "The world-famous Max Sullivan. It's an honor to meet you."

He was way too polite to refuse her handshake, although the sidelong glance he sent in my direction told me I'd have some explaining to do once the two of us were alone. "Very nice to meet you, Ms. Petrucci."

"Alicia," she corrected him, still wearing that Mona Lisa smile of hers. "No need to stand on ceremony."

Because I could tell he wasn't sure how to respond, I said hastily, "Max, why don't you go ahead and sit down? We've got tacos to spare, if you're hungry."

That was for sure. I didn't know which army Alicia had thought she would be feeding, but she'd brought enough takeout from The Skillet to stuff at least a football team and possibly the cheer squad to boot.

Maybe the slightest hesitation after I made the offer. However, this was Max Sullivan, a guy who could sail into just about any social situation and float through it with aplomb, so he said, "That sounds great, especially after all the airplane food I've eaten over the past twelve hours."

"Then go ahead and sit down," I said. "Let me get you a plate and a glass so you can have some water."

This time, his eyebrow lifted just a bit. No, I didn't have wine with every meal, but usually if I had guests, then there was wine on the table.

To my relief, though, he didn't comment, only sat down opposite the spot where Alicia was already seated, placing him on my right side. She'd insisted on me sitting at the head of the table because I was the hostess, and I hadn't bothered to argue the point.

When I came back to the dining room, the two of them were chatting about the weather, a nicely safe topic. As I set down a plate, glass, utensils, and a napkin in front of Max, however, he remarked, "I heard about the latest murder. Are you pulling detective duty on this one?"

I didn't bother to ask how he'd learned about Jessica Rosenthal's death, mostly because I knew he kept in fairly close touch with his mother and I guessed she must have emailed him about the latest murderous goings-on in Las Vegas.

"Um...not really," I hedged, which was only a teeny little lie. After all, I hadn't accomplished much so far, and one slightly oddball dream and a conversation with Justin didn't exactly constitute much of an investigation.

Okay, I'd also done a tea-leaf reading, but again, it hadn't shown me very much.

Was that the slightest flare of surprise in Alicia's expression? She had to be wondering why I hadn't told Max the truth, but because she knew nothing about my true feelings for him...or at least, I prayed she'd remained clueless on that subject...she couldn't know I was still feeling the slightest bit guilty about my aborted date with Justin Hale.

However, it seemed as though Chief DeVargas's interest in my mother as a suspect wasn't yet common knowledge, because otherwise, Max would surely have asked Alicia if she was worried about being a person of interest.

Instead, he commented, "So...you're here in Las Vegas after all these years, Alicia. What brought you back?"

"Skye, of course," she replied, looking imperturbable. "It was time for me to come back into her life."

"Really?" he said, his expression one of simple

interest and nothing more...even if I knew better. "Why's that?"

"Another taco?" I asked desperately.

But because he hadn't eaten all of the ones I'd deposited on his plate a minute earlier, Max saw my delaying tactic for what it was. "Ah...mother/daughter privilege, I guess."

Alicia flicked a glance toward me. Although she hadn't said anything out loud, I could tell she was wondering whether Max knew anything about my magical powers, or whether they were something I preferred to keep on the down-low.

But because he'd been there to witness Tilly talking, and in fact was the first person to encourage me to really develop my magic, I knew this was something I didn't need to hide from him. In fact, at the moment I'd welcome his input, since I honestly didn't know what my next step should be.

"It's okay, Alicia," I said. "He knows."

She lifted her chin, looking thoughtful, even as Max seemed to absorb the way I'd addressed my mother by her first name. My words seemed to signal to him that, even if I might have allowed her back in my life just a little bit, I definitely wasn't ready to launch into a normal mother/daughter relationship with the woman who'd pulled such a disappearing act on me.

"I see," she responded, and drank some water

before turning her attention back to Max. He still looked larger than life as he sat there at the dining room table, skin tanned from his stint in the tropics, his light brown hair a little brighter than I remembered, probably also bleached a bit by the fierce equatorial sun. "In our family—the Petruccis, that is—our magic doesn't come into its full strength until we turn thirty. I came to Las Vegas to talk to Skye about her magic and to make sure she can control it before it develops all the way."

"Oh, she's pretty good at that," Max said, his tone as casual as if we were talking about my latest foray into spinning sugar, or whatever.

I had to mentally thank him for the vote of confidence, even though deep down, I thought it might be a little misplaced. After all, the only real spell he'd ever seen me cast was the one to make Tilly talk, and since he currently would have no reason to believe I'd been able to reverse it, I didn't think that particular spell merited a description of "pretty good."

"She's very good," Alicia said. "Skye, you should show him what you were able to do the other night."

"Oh, I don't think so...." I demurred. While it had been fun to fly around the house with her, I didn't know whether I wanted to perform that kind of aerial acrobatics in front of Max Sullivan. No, it wasn't as if I had to worry about him seeing up my skirt or anything—I was safely wearing skinny jeans tucked into the tall, lug-soled boots I put on whenever it got snowy—but still, something about taking to the air in front of him didn't feel right.

"No, I want to see," he said, his tone coaxing. Then he added, because he could probably tell I was feeling uncomfortable, "I promise I won't freak out or anything."

"Go on, Skye," Alicia put in. "If you haven't hidden your magic from him before this, then I don't see the reason to be shy now."

Easy for her to say. I happened to think there was a huge difference between reading a few tea leaves or even making a cat talk, and flying up into the air like a big dodo bird. But because I had the feeling any further arguments would get shot down, I decided just to go with it.

"All right," I said, and set my napkin on the table as I stood. Even as I rose from my chair, I told myself I didn't have to actually fly anywhere. Probably levitating a few feet would be enough to prove that the magical talents I'd inherited didn't have to follow the laws of gravity.

So that was what I did—allowed myself to float about three feet off the floor, then drift gently sideways in a motion that wasn't exactly flying but still proved I didn't have to stay stuck in one place while I used this newfound skill of mine.

Max's mouth didn't exactly drop open, but it was still pretty obvious that he was properly astonished, judging by the way his eyes widened as he watched my feet leave the oriental rug.

After I'd descended back to solid ground, he said, "How did you find out you could do that?"

"I showed her," Alicia said calmly as she picked up a chicken taco. "It's not that difficult, but it's something that clearly shows magic is at work. Honestly, there isn't a lot she can't do with her magic, as long as it only affects the physical world."

The same thing she'd told me right before Max appeared on my doorstep. In a way, that was freakier than seeing the future in a dream or in the leaves left behind in a teacup. Flying seemed innocuous enough, but what if I wanted to summon fire or decide I was tired of whoever that jerk was who liked to scream down my quiet street at 4 a.m., and have his tires blow out at an extremely inopportune moment?

That kind of magical manipulation sounded downright scary. I didn't want to play God.

"'Anything'?" Max repeated. His tone wasn't skeptical. No, he had that light in his clear blue eyes that told me he was already hatching up some sort of mischief.

Uh-oh.

"Well, within reason," Alicia told him. She probably didn't know him well enough to recognize the shift in his expression for what it was, which I had to count as a good thing. "It's not as though she can stop the rotation of the earth or make the sun rise in the west. But smaller things... most of those should be within the scope of her magic."

"Not that I plan on going all crazy with it," I said firmly.

Again, Max lifted an eyebrow, as though he didn't buy that protest for a minute. However, since he could obviously tell I wasn't in the mood to discuss the subject further—at least, not with Alicia sitting right there—he didn't push it, only said, "Still, it sounds like a good thing to have in your arsenal."

After making that comment, he subtly guided the conversation toward the project he'd just wrapped up in Costa Rica, telling funny stories about the shoot without giving away any real information about the plot of the movie itself. Alicia saw what he was doing, of course, but went along with the change in subject, and then, a bit after eight, said she needed to get back to her hotel.

"The weather report said it might start snowing a little after nine," she told us. "So I figure it's probably best to get off the road before then."

Whether that was entirely the truth, I didn't know, because I hadn't been paying much attention. My old Subaru Outback had all-wheel drive, so as long as the streets weren't completely impass-able—which hardly ever happened—I knew I could make it to the coffee shop without too much trouble, since it was less than a mile away.

But Alicia's fancy BMW coupe definitely didn't have four-wheel-drive or even chains on the tires, so it was probably better for her to be cautious. Max and I got up from the table to walk with her over to the closet so she could retrieve her coat, and she smiled at him.

"It was very nice to meet you, Max," she said. "Just don't get stuck in the snow on your way home."

"Oh, I won't," he replied, looking supremely unconcerned. "My Bronco has four-wheel drive, and I don't have far to go."

That seemed like a slight exaggeration to me. Not about his SUV's four-wheel capability, but the remark that Sunset Ridge wasn't very far away. No, it wasn't as if he'd have to drive all the way to Santa Fe or Taos or something, but still, the ranch lay a good three or four miles from where we stood, and the last part of the trip was over an unpaved gravel lane—a well-maintained one, but still.

But I wasn't going to argue with him. He knew that route a lot better than I did, and since he did a lot of his own stunts...enough that his insurers probably weren't super-happy with him...I guessed he must be able to handle driving over rough roads.

Alicia nodded, wished us both a good night, and then headed out, drawing on a pair of sleek leather gloves as she made her way down the porch steps. I closed the door behind her, then turned to see Max watching me with a speculative gleam in his eyes.

"Okay," he said. "Want to tell me the real reason she was here?"

I could only shake my head. "We already went over that," I replied, hoping the brisk tone in my voice would dissuade him from asking any further questions.

I should have known better.

"Oh, come on, Skye," he returned. "The woman walked out of your life almost thirty years ago, and now you're going to buy her story about coming back to teach you magic?"

"It's the truth," I said, even as the slightest niggle of doubt began to stir in the back of my mind.

What if Alicia had another, darker reason for being here?

I told myself that was ridiculous, that this wasn't some TV show where the backstabbing baby momma resurfaces years later to wreak havoc in her child's life.

As if reappearing to talk about the magic that ran in your family wasn't crazy enough.

I told Max as much, and he only shrugged

before heading back to the table so he could reach for the last of the barbacoa tacos.

"You want this?" he asked, fingers paused above the taco in question as he apparently realized at the last minute that maybe it wasn't polite to scarf up the remaining food without checking to see if it was okay with his host.

"No, you have it," I said, and sat down as well. Now I really wished we had some wine to pour, but since it would probably look weird—or at least desperate—to get out a bottle now, I pushed the thought away as best I could.

"I mean, obviously Chief DeVargas thinks your mother is dodgy," he went on, and I stared at him, wide-eyed.

"How do you know about that?" I demanded. "You didn't say anything a few minutes ago when we were talking."

Or give off any impression at all that he'd heard about the way my mother had been arrested for Jessica Rosenthal's murder. Then again, he was an actor, and a damn good one. He could probably make me think whatever he wanted.

Talk about a scary gift, even if it wasn't actually magic.

"My mom told me," he said, and took a bite of his taco. "She talked to Darcy Montoya, and she told her."

Darcy worked at the police station, and must

have been there to see Alicia do her walk of shame when she was brought in to be booked. I supposed I was probably being naïve to think the story hadn't made the rounds by now, even if no one had had the *cojones* to say something to my face about the way my mother had been arrested.

Doing so would have been extremely rude. My fellow Las Vegans liked to gossip, but they also knew when not to cross a line.

"Chief DeVargas is totally barking up the wrong tree," I responded, and drank some of my water. "She heard about Alicia arguing with Jessica Rosenthal and made some stupid assumptions. Anyway, she obviously wasn't so firm in her convictions that Alicia was denied bail, so there's that."

Maybe Max's mouth compressed ever so slightly. However, he took another look at me and apparently decided it was better not to press the point, because his next words were on an entirely different topic.

"So...done anything else fun with your magic?"

"No," I said severely. "I don't want this to change anything. So I can levitate and maybe fly a little. It's not the most useful magical talent in the world."

"But it'll help you get stuff down from high shelves," he replied with a grin.

Okay, that was true enough. And even though I'd had wistful flying dreams as a child, I didn't see how much practical use that particular skill would be in real life. It wasn't as if I could just fly to work every morning instead of driving my ancient Subaru.

Someone would be sure to notice.

"Alicia said your magic affects physical things," Max went on, obviously undeterred. "So...can you make your vacuum cleaner work without you pushing it? How about having your muffins mix themselves?" His eyes brightened, and he added, "Oh, how about affecting the latest Powerball?"

I stared back at him, not entirely sure whether he was teasing me or not. "That would be cheating," I said primly, and he only grinned back at me.

"Maybe," he allowed. "But...could you?"

Good question. Alicia had said my talent affected physical objects, and those little plastic balls they used to draw the numbers for the Powerball...or most lotteries, when you got right down to it...were definitely physical.

If I hadn't already known I could reach out with my magic and make a bunch of gourds fly around the dining room, I might have tried a little mental push right then, just to check for myself. But I knew I was able to do that much, so I didn't really see the point.

What Max had just suggested, though, was an order of magnitude different. He was talking about using my magic to affect something miles away from me, a feat that felt like a whole other ball of wax.

I said as much, and the eager glint in his blue eyes didn't waver for a moment.

"Well, that's easy enough to find out," he told me. "Why don't you try moving something in your shop, and then we can drive over there and see if you really made it work."

The thought of getting in Max's Bronco and driving across town in the snow and cold—four-wheel-drive notwithstanding—didn't appeal to me very much. At the same time, though, it seemed like a simple enough test of whether my magic could reach across a distance like that and still have any effect.

And anything that would allow me to spend more time with Max Sullivan was always a good idea.

"Okay," I said, then added on an impulse, "but if I make this work, then you have to buy me a drink at the Plaza afterward."

"Deal," Max replied at once. Mouth quirking, he added, "I was kind of bummed to see you didn't have a bottle of wine open or some beers out or something."

"Magic and alcohol don't mix," I informed him.

"Maybe they don't," he said, then paused, one eyebrow cocking at an angle I recognized all too well. "But you'll be doing your magic before we go out for drinks, so it's all good, right?"

I had to hope so. Right then, I was just glad that the Plaza's bar stayed open until eleven even on Sunday evenings.

But it wasn't nearly that late, and I knew I'd have to stop after the one drink, since I had to be up at four-thirty the next morning. All the same, I had to admit I was eager to see whether my magic really would be able to affect a physical object almost a mile away from where I currently stood.

Something easy, though, an item that wouldn't cause too much of a disruption to my business in case this little experiment went sideways.

That ruled out any silly tricks with my Breville espresso maker, which I really couldn't afford to replace. Ditto for the heavy cast-iron baking sheets I used to bake my croissants.

But no one would have too much of a problem if one of the napkin dispensers I had sitting on a table decided to fly through the air and land on the counter. I told Max about my plan, and he nodded.

"Sounds great. Let's go check it out."

I set one hand on my hip. "I have to do the magic first—and I'm not tearing out of here and leaving all this stuff on the table."

Was that an eye roll?

It sure looked like it, but at least he didn't

argue, and only said, "Okay, you do your thing, and I'll take the plates into the kitchen. Deal?"

"Deal," I said, knowing my mouth quirked a bit as I made the reply.

He went ahead and gathered up the plates, and then stacked the takeout bag on top. Once he'd disappeared down the hall into the kitchen, I figured it was time to try my little trick.

I really had no idea how any of this worked, but Alicia had told me more than once that the Petrucci magic was all about focusing your will on an object, an idea, or even yourself.

And that's exactly what I did.

In my mind's eye, I imagined the metal holder with its complement of paper napkins, how it was sitting on the little round table closest to the display case that usually held pastries and crois- sants, although that case would be empty now, waiting until I came to work tomorrow morning to fill it once again.

Maybe if I'd really wanted to challenge myself, I would've chosen a holder on the table that was farthest from the counter, but I figured it was prob- ably better to start with baby steps.

And then I imagined the napkin holder floating into the air and quietly sailing across the darkened space before landing on the bit of marble counter between the cash register and the display case.

That was easy enough. Now I'd just have to see whether it really worked or not.

Max emerged from the kitchen and sent me a questioning look. "Well?"

"I did it," I said. "Or at least, I did it in my mind. Whether it worked in real life is anyone's guess."

"We're about to find out. Come on."

Of course, we couldn't head right out the door, because we both had to pause to put on our jackets and hats before stepping into the frigid night. Even sheltered as I was by the porch roof, little puffs of vapor escaped my lips when we stopped once again so I could lock the front door.

However, it wasn't snowing yet, although the sky overhead felt heavier and lower than usual, just waiting to release its complement of icy flakes. I could only hope we'd get this mission handled— and our drinks consumed—before it really decided to let go.

But soon enough we were safely inside Max's Bronco, with the seats already starting to heat up as he pulled away from the curb. Not for the first time, I reflected that I really did need to see about getting a new car at some point. Maybe not one with all the bells and whistles like the vehicle I rode in now, but something that could give me heated seats in the winter and reliable air conditioning in the summer. Yes, my Subaru had A/C, but it only worked when it felt like it…which had been less and less frequently over the past couple of years.

Neither one of us said much on the short drive over to the Plaza. That was fine, though; it felt just about perfect to be sitting in the car with Max, to realize he really was back from Costa Rica and that I didn't have to worry about him going off on an extended trip any time soon. His next movie wasn't slated to start shooting until late June, and although he often had to slip away for a business trip here and there, those jaunts never lasted more than a day or two at the most, not the interminable six weeks-plus that this latest movie had demanded. And while some people might have wondered how the guy could have that much energy to spare after a twelve-hour plane trip, my only response would be that they'd obviously never met Max Sullivan.

On a Sunday evening that threatened snow, the parking around Las Vegas's downtown plaza wasn't exactly in high demand. Max was able to get one of the spots right in front of the hotel, probably figuring he should park there, since that was where we were going to end up.

It felt kind of strange to enter Levitation Latte via the front door. Whenever I came to work, I parked in one of the spots in back and came in via the kitchen/storeroom. This time, though, there wasn't much point in doing that, considering how we'd left Max's Bronco in front of the Plaza.

All was dark inside the shop, except for one light I always left on in the little hallway where the bathroom was located. I went over to the switch and turned on the overhead lamps above the bar/display case.

There was the napkin holder, sitting right where I'd sent it with my mind.

A little shiver went through me that didn't have anything to do with the frosty outside air.

Max gave me a questioning glance. "Is that it?"

"Yes," I said. "Right where I wanted it to go."

A pleased smile tugged at his lips. "Well, I guess that's your answer."

About all I could do was nod. But even though he seemed to think the experiment had been a raging success, I still harbored a few doubts.

"I got it to move," I told him. "And I'll admit that's pretty cool. But my house is less than a mile from here. We don't know how far I can stretch my powers."

"True," Max admitted, although he still looked cheerful. "Maybe try another experiment?"

I got the feeling he'd be happy to keep this up all night. With the way the weather was threatening, however, I didn't think it was a very good idea to try messing around with stuff that would require us to drive miles and miles to find out whether or not my latest magical test had had the same results.

"Not tonight," I said firmly, in tones I hoped would let him know I was done for the evening. "We tried the experiment, and it worked. Let's leave it there for now, okay?"

For the briefest second, it looked as though Max wanted to argue. But then he seemed to take a good look at my expression and decide he'd better let it go. "Sure," he replied. "Let's get that drink."

A drink sounded like a great idea. I nodded, and we went outside so I could lock up again and engage the alarm. Those tasks accomplished, we hurried inside the hotel just as the first few flakes of snow started to fall.

"I'm still kind of hungry," Max said as we headed for one of the tables near the window. "You mind if I order some truffle fries or something?"

"Of course not," I replied, then added with a smile, "As long as I can steal a couple."

He grinned back at me. "I think I can manage that."

Since he'd been almost a full-time resident of Las Vegas for nearly six months by that point, people here weren't as starstruck when they bumped into Max now as they might have been back in September after he first arrived on the scene. The woman working behind the counter that night—Leila Moreno, who'd been two years behind me in high school—came over and said, "What can I get you?"

"A couple of tempranillos and some truffle fries," Max responded at once.

Under normal circumstances, I might have been annoyed by a man trying to order a glass of wine for me. But the two of us had gotten a drink here enough times that he knew which of the wines offered at the bar I liked the most, and his doing so now just streamlined the whole process.

Leila headed off to get our drinks and place our truffle fries order with the kitchen, which was actually located across the hall that divided the ground floor of the building, in the hotel's restaurant proper. Except for one couple nursing their drinks at the bar, Max and I were the only people in the room that night. No big surprise, considering it was edging past eight-thirty on a Sunday night with a storm threatening the town.

"So...you're really done with the Costa Rica project?" I asked, and he nodded. Although he'd told Alicia and me funny stories about the shoot, he hadn't actually said whether he was home for good or whether he might have to head back to film a few pick-up scenes.

"Yeah, finally. Costa Rica is beautiful, but that last week or so, I could only think about heading home."

"To buy some horses," I responded, only halfway joking.

"At some point," he said. He had to pause the

conversation there, since Leila had come back with our wine, but after she was gone, he added, "I mean, it's not going to be prime riding weather for a while, so I might hold off until it gets warmer. It's on the list, though."

I wanted to ask him what else was on the "list," but feared he might think I was being a little too nosy. While we shared a lot more confidences than most people probably expected, it wasn't as though he told me everything about what was going on in his life...or vice versa.

"Well, here's to being back in Las Vegas," I said, and he lifted his glass and clinked it against mine so we could both take a belated sip.

"It feels good to be back." He paused there and glanced around the nearly empty bar. "Doesn't look like much has changed since I left."

Considering he'd hopped on that first plane to Costa Rica only six weeks earlier, that definitely wasn't enough time for our hometown to have changed materially. "You'd need to give it about six years for there to have been any changes you could actually notice," I joked, but Max didn't smile in return and instead looked uncharacteristically serious.

"True. That's probably one of the things I like most about the place. You don't feel like you're on a hamster wheel, always running to keep up."

I lifted an eyebrow, thinking that comment

didn't sound very much like the man I knew. He'd always been the first to want to try new things, to get out and have some kind of new adventure.

"No hamster wheels around here," I said lightly, and now he did smile.

"Not many, anyway."

Leila arrived with the truffle fries right then, and we both paused for a minute so Max could help himself to a few—and make sure he told me I was welcome to as many as I wanted.

But I'd eaten my fill of tacos just an hour before, and so was fine with stealing a single fry here and there, just as I'd warned him I might do.

"Who do you think really killed Jessica Rosenthal?" he asked when we broke for another sip of wine.

Surprised, I could only stare back at him and give a helpless lift of my shoulders. "I have no idea. I just know that Alicia couldn't have done it. Unfortunately, there don't seem to be many likely suspects."

Being Max, he didn't look too dismayed by my comment. "Well," he said. "Once you've exhausted the likely suspects, it's time to move on to the unlikely ones. Did you do a tea-leaf reading about it?"

"I did," I replied. There didn't seem much point in beating around the bush, since I'd already known he was going to ask the question sooner or later. "But the only clue I got was a heart, which didn't help at all. Whatever else is going on here, it doesn't sound like Jessica was killed by a jealous lover or anything like that. I've been wracking my brains trying to figure out what it could possibly mean and coming up with nothing."

His expression turned sympathetic. "I know it's frustrating," he said. "You've always found the killer in the past, though, so I don't see any reason why you won't find him this time, too."

That observation sounded awfully optimistic to me, but I didn't bother to argue with him. So, I'd gotten lucky a couple of times. That didn't mean my luck would necessarily hold out this particular go-'round.

I shrugged and sipped some more wine, and he said, "Maybe you should do a second tea-leaf reading."

My mouth twisted. "Because I had such great luck the first time."

"Hey, you never know."

No, I didn't. And he was right—sometimes I needed to have another round with the tea leaves to see if there was something else the universe wanted to tell me.

Not tonight, though. After we were done with this drink, I was letting Max drive me home and then basically falling into bed after that. The tea leaves would have to wait until the following afternoon.

I told him I'd give it a try after I got home from work the next day, and he, gauging my mood, obviously decided he'd better let it go. Instead, we talked a little more about his film shoot and about his plans to fix up the stables on his property.

Anything except Jessica Rosenthal's murder, and the lack of any viable suspects.

The snow was falling a little more thickly as we left the bar, but not so hard that I had to worry about Max getting me home safely. However, he insisted on walking me up to the front door and making sure I was inside and the deadbolt engaged before he turned and headed back to his SUV.

No goodnight kiss, obviously, not even an attempt at one. By that point, I shouldn't have been surprised, but I still couldn't hold back my disappointment as I headed up the stairs so I could get ready for bed.

It sure looked as though absence hadn't made Max's heart grow any fonder.

CHAPTER 11

Ex Hex

G ood thing I'd only had that one glass of wine with Max, because I had a feeling I would've been even groggier when I wandered downstairs at o'dark thirty the next morning after showering and getting dressed. It was way too black outside to see exactly what the weather was doing, but after I flicked on the light above the back stoop, I could see that at least three inches of snow had fallen the night before, maybe a little more.

And that meant I had to shovel the driveway before I could get out.

Trying not to curse under my breath...and not succeeding very well...I pushed open the garage door and got out the shovel, which at least had been propped up against the wall near the door and didn't require me to dig through mounds of my grandmother's belongings in order to find it.

All the same, by the time I had the driveway cleared and was on my way to work, I was already feeling grumpier than usual. No, Mondays weren't my favorite day of the week, since having to wake up so early after sleeping in until seven on Saturday and Sunday always felt like a shock no matter how often I did it, but still.

One thing that did cheer me up slightly was seeing Tilly curled up in her bed when I came into the kitchen/storeroom space at the back of the shop. She'd refused to come home with me that weekend, and I'd put out extra food and water for her, and hadn't turned down the thermostat quite as much as I might otherwise have if I'd known the cat was going to spend Saturday and Sunday at my house.

She cracked a green eye as I unwrapped the scarf from around my throat and then paused to adjust the thermostat upward a couple of degrees to its usual wintertime seventy. "Some of us are trying to sleep."

"And some of us have to get to work," I returned, doing my best not to sound too irritated. "How was your weekend?"

"Uneventful." Apparently deciding that trying to sleep any more was a lost cause, she got up and stretched, back arching and tail waving from side to side. "But it was nice to be able to stay here instead of going to your house."

"I thought you said you liked my house," I replied, wondering whether I should feel wounded by her comment or not. The cat had a bed in a cozy corner of the living room and free run of the backyard when she came to my place, so it wasn't as though I was locking her up in a bathroom or something.

"It's fine. But it's not nearly as interesting to wander around your neighborhood."

No, probably not. I loved where I lived, loved all the old houses that had been so carefully restored and the big trees that lined the street, but for a cat who was used to roaming around downtown and poking her nose into dumpsters filled by the various restaurants and businesses located there, it had to be hopelessly dull.

"Well, I'm glad you had a good weekend," I said mildly, and then headed out to the main part of the coffee shop so I could get the day's first batch of brew going. Technically, I could've started it a little later, since I wouldn't be opening for another hour and a half, but I tended to wait until I got to work to have my first shot of caffeine and knew I needed it this morning ASAP.

But once the coffee was brewing, I headed back to the kitchen and started mixing up some cranberry, blueberry, and banana nut muffin batter, as well as putting together the dough for some croissants, both plain and filled with ham and Swiss cheese. A quick detour out to the front of the shop to pour my first cup of the morning, and after a few sips, I started to feel almost human.

Deanne arrived just after I finished my cup. "I heard Max is back in town," she said, not bothering with her customary Monday morning greeting.

"Yes, he stopped by last night," I replied. My tone was casual, although I guessed it probably didn't fool my best friend for even a second.

"And?" Her expression was way too hopeful.

"And nothing," I said.

Undeterred, she said, "But you two went out for drinks at the hotel last night."

"A single glass of wine," I responded. Again, no point in asking how she'd learned that Max and I had gone to the hotel bar for some wine the night before. Deanne's house might have been located on the opposite end of town from the Plaza Hotel, but Las Vegas's gossip network knew no bounds. "And that was only because I told him I needed it as a reward after performing a little experiment."

"'Experiment'?" she repeated, now looking confused.

As quickly as I could, I explained what I'd learned over the past couple of days about my magic, and how I'd been able to reach out from a distance to move the napkin dispenser from a table to the counter. "But it's really no big deal," I concluded, even as Deanne lifted an eyebrow.

"No big deal to move something with your mind when you're almost a mile away? I'd say that was a super-big deal."

"It's just parlor tricks," I said.

She looked far from convinced, but since she could tell I really didn't want to talk about it anymore, she didn't press me on the subject, only headed out into the coffee shop proper so she could get a pot of decaf going and then take care of the rest of her early-morning tasks, like making sure all the sugar and cinnamon shakers were filled and that there was adequate toilet paper in the bathroom.

I had a feeling she didn't plan to let the matter go completely, however, but was only biding her time until the opportunity to circle back 'round to the subject presented itself.

Well, I'd worry about that when the time came.

Despite the snow on the ground—or maybe because of it—we were busy that morning, with barely a chance to catch our breaths until well past the witching hour of nine-thirty when the early rush usually began to die down. Even then, we still had people coming and going through late morning, although not at the same frantic pace as we'd experienced earlier.

That whole time, I kept hoping Kyle would appear so I could try to pick his brain about Jessica Rosenthal's murder. No, he wasn't really supposed to discuss that kind of stuff with me, but he'd ignored that rule in the past, and so I had no reason to believe he wouldn't ignore it now.

Problem was, I didn't see hide nor hair of him, which was frustrating, to say the least. My relationship with Kyle could be fraught, considering how he'd never quite given up on the hope that one day I'd realize I'd made a mistake in breaking up with him and would ask to take him back, but he was definitely my best resource when it came to learning how the Las Vegas P.D. was handling a particular investigation.

A little before eleven, a man who looked vaguely familiar came in to the shop. He was probably in his late thirties, with the sort of lean, long-nosed face that was interesting without being handsome. After asking for a cup of black coffee and a plain croissant—a duplicate of the order he'd placed before, I realized, remembering that he'd come in during the midmorning rush on Friday—he headed over to sit down at a table off in one corner.

Something about him piqued my interest, although I couldn't really say why. It wasn't as though we didn't get plenty of tourists passing through Las Vegas and even spending a few days here, although generally, a snowy Monday that wasn't part of a holiday weekend didn't tend to attract a lot of visitors.

I only knew the stranger wasn't part of the *Fix My Town* team, or at least, if he was, then he'd hadn't arrived in town with the rest of the crew, for whatever reason.

Deanne hadn't spared the stranger much more than a casual glance, though, telling me that while he might have pinged my radar for some reason, he definitely wasn't anyone she thought she needed to waste any time on.

After sending a glance in his direction to make sure he wasn't listening to us—he didn't appear to be, and instead had his gaze fixed on his phone's screen as he sipped coffee and absent-mindedly munched on his croissant—Deanne said in an undertone, "What are you going to do about it?"

"Do about what?" I responded.

She let out a long-suffering sigh. "What we were talking about before," she said, now sounding annoyed. "I mean, you're going to keep experimenting with it, aren't you?"

"I don't know," I said, which was the simple truth. Although I hadn't done anything too crazy with my magic yet, knowing I had that kind of power buried inside me made me feel more than a little uneasy. So far it seemed fairly well-behaved...at least, it hadn't decided to go crazy and send a tornado spinning down Bridge Street or topple all the trees in Plaza Park...but that didn't mean it couldn't. I added, since it seemed obvious my friend wanted more of an answer than what I'd given her, "Right now, I feel like it's probably a better idea to let sleeping magic powers lie."

"You are such a stick in the mud," Deanne complained.

That remark earned her some serious side-eye from me, because I definitely didn't see myself that way. All right, I wasn't a wild-child party girl—it was kind of hard to be that sort of person in sleepy Las Vegas, New Mexico, especially with a job that required me to wake up when most party animals would just be getting ready for bed—but I was usually up for some fun as long as it didn't sound too crazy.

Hmm...maybe I was a stick in the mud.

"I just don't want to accidentally blow up Bridge Street or something," I said, still speaking in a lower tone of voice than I normally would. The guy at the table across the room didn't seem to be paying any particular attention to Deanne and me, but this wasn't exactly a topic I wanted overheard by anyone. The only people in Las Vegas who knew my magic extended to anything more than reading tea leaves were Max, Alicia, and Deanne—well, and Tilly, I supposed—and I needed to make sure it stayed that way. "And I was going to talk to Alicia tonight about what I did yesterday evening. I just haven't had a chance to send her a text to see whether she's available or not."

No reason why she shouldn't be...it wasn't as if she knew a lot of people here in town...but at the same time, I didn't want to make assumptions. However, all morning I'd been thinking that I really did need to talk to her again and find out whether what I'd done was at all unusual, or whether using magic on objects from afar was the sort of thing Petrucci witches had mastered from the time they were little kids.

The door opened and Kyle walked in. I brightened for a moment, thinking I was finally going to have a chance to pick his brain about Jessica Rosenthal's murder, until I realized he wasn't alone, and instead had one of his fellow deputies—Cody Rivera—with him. Neither one of them spared a single glance at Deanne and me where we stood behind the counter, but instead walked over to the man who was sitting at the table across the room with his half-drunk cup of coffee and half-eaten croissant.

"Elliott Rosenthal?" Kyle said clearly, his voice carrying across the room. The man nodded, and Kyle went on, sounding way more brisk and professional than I'd ever heard him before, "You're under arrest for the murder of Jessica Rosenthal. You have the right to remain silent. Anything you say can be used against you in court. You have the right to talk to a lawyer for advice before we ask you any questions. You have the right to have a lawyer with you during questioning. If you cannot afford a lawyer, one will be appointed for you before any questioning if you wish. If you decide to answer questions now without a lawyer present, you have the right to stop answering at any time." He paused there and added, "Do you understand these rights?"

"Yes," the man said, sounding resigned. "But I'm not your guy."

This almost off-hand protestation of innocence didn't seem to have much effect on either of the deputies. Kyle said, "Please stand."

Well, at least he'd said "please."

The man took one last bite of his croissant and a final swallow of Italian roast, and then got to his feet. He was tall and slim, almost lanky, a good inch or two taller than the men who'd come to arrest him. However, he didn't seem inclined to present any sort of a threat, and only put his hands behind him so Kyle could clasp a pair of handcuffs around his wrists.

Then the deputies marched the man out of the store, with Kyle sending me just the briefest glance before they headed outside, as though to tell me he'd try to explain later when he wasn't on official business.

After the door closed behind them, Deanne looked over at me, eyes wide. "What was that all about?"

"I don't know," I said. "I guess they gathered some new evidence. But did you hear the guy's name?"

She gave a nod. "Elliott Rosenthal. Jessica's husband?"

About all I could do was lift my shoulders. "Maybe," I replied, even as I thought Jessica hadn't seemed like the sort of person who would keep her husband's name after a divorce.

But it seemed plausible enough that she might have enough IMDB credits under her belt as "Jessica Rosenthal" that it would have been a real pain to have them changed to her maiden name. Since I didn't have an IMDB account, I had no idea how those sorts of things worked.

Max might know, although I had to believe it was the sort of thing his assistant or manager would handle. Well, I'd just make a mental note to ask him later.

"So...does this mean Alicia is off the hook?" Deanne asked next.

A very good question. If the Las Vegas police had enough evidence to arrest this Elliott Rosenthal person, whoever he turned out to be, then it seemed to me they must think my mother couldn't have murdered Jessica.

The only way I'd know for sure, though, would be to contact my mother and see what she had to say.

I reached under the counter so I could pull out my phone and see if I had any missed calls or texts, but there wasn't anything except a quick text from Max that he'd sent the night before, one which simply said, *Home safe.*

But there was nothing after that one, which I'd seen right before I went to bed.

Well, there could be a hundred explanations as to why Alicia hadn't contacted me. For one thing, just because Kyle and Cody had marched in here and arrested this Elliott Rosenthal on the spot, it didn't necessarily mean they'd notified my mother that she was no longer a suspect and therefore her bail had been canceled.

Or maybe she was still a suspect, just not as high on the list as Mr. Rosenthal. I had to admit I was kind of hazy as to how all this worked.

Whatever was going on, I figured it couldn't hurt to send her a quick text. It was almost eleven o'clock by that point, so even if she was a super-late sleeper, no one could claim that I'd violated protocol by reaching out way too early in the morning.

"I don't know," I told Deanne. "But I'm going to text her now and see if she's no longer a suspect, or if she even knows what's going on."

"Sounds like a plan."

We didn't have a chance to say anything more than that, because the door to the coffee shop opened, and a couple of women who I guessed were part of the *Fix My Town* team entered the space. One of them was very pretty, maybe six years or so younger than Deanne and me, with long, light brown hair and big hazel eyes. The other woman was probably ten years older, with short hair dyed bright blue and a piercing in her nose.

Neither one of the pair looked exactly broken up by Jessica Rosenthal's death, cementing my suspicion that she hadn't been popular on the set. However, since it didn't sound as though the Las Vegas P.D. had arrested any of the crew or even done much questioning of them beyond the bare minimum, apparently no one on the *Fix My Town* team had had a big enough beef with her to take care of the problem in the most final way possible.

The two women put in a large order, eight drinks total, which told me they must be buying for some of the crew, maybe the bunch who were working on the theater, since I knew that particular team was smaller than the crew that was focused on redoing the cowboy emporium.

It was nice to sell so many coffees and lattes at what would usually have been a dead hour of the day, in between the morning and lunch rushes. All the same, getting everything prepped took enough time that when I came up for air and was able to pull out my phone again, I saw I'd missed a text from Alicia.

Apparently, great minds thought alike.

The police just let me know they've arrested another subject & the charges against me are being dropped. Are you free tonight? I'd like to celebrate before I head back to New York.

As I read those words, a pang of disappointment went through me. No, I hadn't expected her to stay here forever, but at the same time, it almost sounded as though she'd only stuck around as long as she had because of the conditions of her bail.

Nice way to make me feel wanted.

Well, what did you expect? I thought then. *She abandoned you for almost thirty years. Did you really think she was going to be all family togetherness now?*

No, probably not.

Still, the news of her imminent departure stung, even though I'd told myself back when all this started that I shouldn't get my hopes up about having any kind of a real relationship with my mother. Yes, I'd let her show me how to use the magic I'd inherited, but....

But I had a feeling Alicia had shown me the ropes, so to speak, because she'd been worried about what might happen as my supposedly momentous thirtieth birthday approached and I still had no idea to use the Petrucci magic. More than anything else, she'd probably just wanted to make sure she covered her butt and that my magic was controlled enough that she wouldn't have to worry about me attracting any undue attention.

Of course I was free that night. My social life wasn't exactly what you could call lively, especially during the week.

Because Max hadn't said anything to me about getting together this evening, I figured it was safe to get back to her quickly.

Sure, I'm free. What time?

Meet me at the restaurant at The Castañeda at 7?

An echo of my dinner date with Justin last week. I had to hope this particular meal wouldn't come to quite such a crashing halt.

That works, I wrote. *See you then.*

She responded with a smiley emoji, and that seemed to be that.

I put my phone away, and looked up to see Deanne watching me.

"Was that Max?" she asked.

Talk about a one-track mind. Yes, I wanted more than anything to be with him, but I definitely wasn't going to push things and run the risk of losing our friendship.

Whereas Deanne seemed to think that if we just spent enough time together, sooner rather than later he'd wake up and realize his soul mate had been waiting for him here in Las Vegas all along.

"No," I said evenly. "It was Alicia. The police have dropped the murder charges, and she's going to be heading back to New York. She wanted to have dinner before she left."

At once, my friend's lips thinned. I could tell she felt vindicated now that Alicia had pretty much proved she had no intention of becoming a permanent part of my life.

And I tried to tell myself that was okay. I'd gotten along just fine without her for twenty-nine years, and I was sure I'd get along fine for the next twenty-nine, too.

However, something in my expression must have told Deanne this wasn't the time for "I told you so," because she tilted her head slightly and said, "It's good to hear the police have dropped the charges."

Yes, that was definitely a relief.

But as I headed over to grind a fresh batch of beans for the inevitable lunch rush of coffee drinkers, I couldn't help wondering whether Elliott Rosenthal had been telling the truth when Kyle and Cody arrested him.

Because if Alicia wasn't guilty and neither was Elliott, then who was the real killer?

CHAPTER 12

Rumspringa

Nothing much of note happened the rest of that day, although I did get a text from Justin in the afternoon just a few minutes before Deanne and I started closing up the coffee shop right around three-thirty.

It's been crazy. But I'd still like to try to have dinner again. Maybe Wednesday night?

Well, that was convenient. No way would he want to go on a first date—or maybe I should call it Date 1.5, since we'd at least tried before—on Valentine's Day, which was tomorrow.

I told myself that was fine. Honestly, I'd only been trying to have a little fun with Justin while he was in town, and definitely wasn't looking for a relationship.

Also, I could only hope that if Max found out I'd been on a date with someone from the *Fix My*

Town crew, maybe he'd get just the teeniest bit jealous.

I decided I'd better write back before I could try to second-guess myself.

The Castañeda again?

Let's meet at The Skillet.

Not nearly as fancy, but I loved the food, so I wouldn't argue.

Sure. 7 again?

That works.

With the matter settled, I returned my phone to my apron pocket and went back to rinsing out one of the coffee carafes. Deanne, all eagle eyes, obviously hadn't missed the way I'd been texting.

"I hope that wasn't Alicia canceling on you," she said, in tones that boded ill for my mother if she was looking for an easy way to flake out on our meeting tonight.

"No," I said, my voice even. "That was Justin, asking if we could try having dinner again. So I said sure."

"Tomorrow?"

"No," I said again. "On Wednesday."

She didn't quite humph, but I could tell from the way her mouth twisted ever so slightly that she thought he was chicken for purposely avoiding taking me out to dinner on Valentine's Day.

If that was even what was going on. For all I knew, he was going to be working late tomorrow and just wouldn't be available until the following day. Since I hadn't been paying a huge amount of attention to how the work was progressing on the various projects the *Fix My Town* team had going around Las Vegas, I really didn't know what his days even looked like.

And I hadn't forgotten my conversation with Max the night before, and how I'd promised I would do another tea-leaf reading today and see if anything more helpful turned up. At the moment, I wasn't feeling too sanguine about my prospects, but I'd said I would do it, and that meant I needed to perform the ritual no matter what my personal feelings on the subject might be. Some people might have said there wasn't much point in continuing to pick at the problem, since Alicia now appeared to be off the hook, and yet I didn't like unanswered questions, even setting aside my promise to Max.

The snow was long gone, but the day was still cold and gray, the kind of weather that seemed right for brewing a cup of tea and sitting down to enjoy it. That was why, after I got home, I made oolong instead of the gunpowder green tea I usually brewed for this purpose, and why I lingered at the kitchen table longer than I normally would have, sipping from the antique teacup and staring at the snow-covered garden outside.

However, I didn't let my thoughts drift so

much that I couldn't hold the all-important central question in my mind.

Who killed Jessica Rosenthal...and why?

When the cup was finally drained, I placed its saucer on top and inverted them both, letting the last tiny bits of liquid drip their way down from the cup. Then I turned it right-side up and peered inside.

This time, there was almost no residue stuck to the side, except one blob almost directly in front of me that looked like a hand, if a chubby one. For a long second, I stared at it, wondering what the leaves were trying to tell me this time. Yes, someone must have used their hands to tighten that phone charging cord around Jessica's neck, but I had to believe something else was going on here.

Okay, time to focus on the basics and see if that helped any. In tea-leaf reading, a hand generally meant strength and friendship, charity. In this case, though, the hand was pointing downward, indicating failure, or possibly someone's fortunes taking a downturn.

Well, Jessica Rosenthal had experienced the worst downturn possible...and yet I couldn't help thinking the leaves were trying to tell me something different, something that just wasn't obvious to me, for whatever reason.

But at least I'd gotten a clear symbol, even if I didn't yet know what it meant.

I got up from the kitchen table, washed the cup and saucer by hand, and wondered if I should text Max and let him know what I'd seen. Almost as soon as the thought passed through my mind, however, I dismissed it. There wasn't any point in telling him about the hand if I wasn't sure of its significance. Better to wait until I knew a little more.

That was why, instead of picking up my phone, I climbed the stairs to my bedroom so I could get out of my work clothes and ready for my dinner with Alicia. Nothing hugely fancy, just jeans and a sweater and boots, but at least they were newish and presentable, whereas the black top and faded jeans that were my usual work uniform didn't seem quite appropriate for The Castañeda, even when they weren't smudged with flour and coffee spills.

Changing my clothes and tidying my hair and makeup only took about a half hour, though, which was why I found myself on my laptop afterward, searching online to see if there were any obscure meanings attached to images of hands in tea-leaf readings that I'd forgotten or never heard of before.

I didn't find anything useful, though, so after about forty minutes or maybe a little more, I stopped searching, closed up the laptop, and headed downstairs to watch TV until it was time to head out.

The clouds had parted just enough to the west that I spied a brooding, reddish glow behind the Sangre de Cristo mountains, a sight that didn't do much to improve my mood. Right then, my quiet little Las Vegas looked as though it was perched on the outskirts of Mordor.

But everything was warm and friendly inside the hotel, and Alicia was already waiting for me at a cozy table off in one corner, a place where it was almost guaranteed no one would be able to overhear our conversation. She smiled as I approached, and said, "I'm so glad you could make it tonight, Skye. I need to be on the road early tomorrow."

Just can't wait to get out of here, can you? I thought, although I did my best to return her smile, then sat down in the chair opposite hers. "You're driving all the way to New York?"

"Oh, yes," she said, not looking at all daunted by the prospect of making a journey of some two thousand miles on her own during the winter. "I'm going to take I-40 most of the way and avoid the worst of the weather...I hope. But I drive almost everywhere if I'm traveling domestically. I like to have my own car with me."

Considering that the car in question was a brand-new 7 Series, I supposed I could see why she might feel that way. "It must have been a huge relief to have the charges dropped," I commented, then reached for the glass of water sitting at my place setting.

"It would have blown over one way or another," she responded, still appearing cheery and not at all concerned about the way she might have ended up on trial for first-degree murder. Maybe she'd consulted her own tea leaves regarding the problem, even though she'd claimed having the Sight was more an O'Malley thing, not a Petrucci talent. "But that's not what I wanted to talk to you about."

"Oh?"

A waiter approached us then—someone I didn't recognize and therefore guessed must be a fairly recent transplant to Las Vegas—and asked if we'd like anything to drink. Alicia ordered a glass of merlot, so I did the same thing. Obviously, a bottle wasn't in the offing tonight.

Which made sense, since she had a long drive ahead of her the next morning. The waiter told us he'd back with our drinks in a few minutes, and Alicia picked up her menu after he walked away from the table so she could peruse its contents.

"Might as well get all the business taken care of up front," she said cheerfully. "That way, we won't be interrupted as much."

A sound plan, I supposed, although I couldn't help feeling even more uneasy as to precisely why she'd thought it so important to meet for one last dinner before she left town. It sure sounded to me like she didn't have any particular plans to be a regular part of my life going forward, so what did it matter if we saw each other this final night of her trip to Las Vegas?

I didn't ask. No, I just planned to grit my teeth and endure this, and then, after she was safely away, driving solo along the interstate as she returned to the life she'd left behind, I'd maybe sit down and try to figure out how I really felt about the whole situation.

The waiter came back with our wine, and because we'd both studied the menu during his absence, we ordered quickly, lemon ricotta ravioli for her and roasted chicken—which I knew as excellent—for me. After our server departed, Alicia raised her glass and said, "To Las Vegas."

It seemed like an odd little toast, although maybe she'd meant it in the context of the way the town had been a safe place for me to grow up... mostly safe, at least. No, I hadn't come to any real harm, of course, had only had to deal with some bullying from the mean girls, which definitely didn't make me a special case. It was the sort of thing that happened to thousands—or maybe even millions—of kids who didn't quite fit in.

"To Las Vegas," I echoed, and clinked my glass against hers, then took a sip of wine. It was excellent, fruit-forward without being overpowering, and something I thought would work well with both the dishes we'd ordered.

Alicia also swallowed some wine, a bigger mouthful than I'd allowed myself. Then she said, "I have a confession to make."

Only one? I thought, although I only tipped my head toward her and replied, "What's that?"

"There is no prophecy," she said flatly, and my eyes widened, even as my stomach felt like she'd punched me in the gut while delivering that flabbergasting statement.

"*What?*"

"I made it up," she said, and at least had the grace to look embarrassed, her eyes not quite meeting mine. "I had to think of something to explain why it took me so long to come back here and see you."

Anger churned inside me, but I wouldn't let my rage grow out of control, much as I might have wanted it to. For one thing, even though our table was fairly private, we were still in a public place, and making a scene didn't seem like a very good idea. Besides, if I blew up at Alicia now, I might never get the answer to my next question.

"So...why *did* it take so long?"

Her gaze slid away from mine and to the other occupants of the dining room—all four of them, two couples whose attention appeared to be entirely on one another and not on the mother-daughter pair seated a distance away from them. Apparently satisfied that anything we said wouldn't be overheard, she responded, "Because I was a coward. I knew I needed to talk to you, to try to explain what had happened, but every time I thought I had the nerve to do it, something came up that kept me away. You know how it goes—the longer you put off something you've been dreading, the worse it seems in your mind."

"So...you were dreading seeing me?"

All things considered, I thought I'd sounded pretty calm as I asked the question.

"Not seeing you, my dear, but having to explain myself to you." Her fingers wrapped around the stem of her wine glass, and she lifted it to her lips and took a swallow that lowered the level of liquid inside by at least half an inch. "Have you ever heard of the *rumspringa?*"

The word sounded vaguely familiar, as though I might have heard or read it somewhere before. For the life of me, though, I couldn't remember what it was supposed to mean.

"Not really," I said.

She didn't seem too put off by my ignorance, and sipped a bit more wine before she returned her glass to the tabletop. "It's a thing in Amish communities."

"You're Amish?" I blurted, even as I realized what a silly question that was. Last I checked, the

Amish didn't drive around in expensive European sedans or carry the latest iPhone.

"No," she replied, and though a corner of her mouth might have quirked the littlest bit, I could tell she was trying to quell the impulse to smile outright at my ignorance. "I suppose the best way to explain it is that the Petruccis have sort of adopted the custom over the years. The *rumspringa* is a time when young people—usually in their late teens but sometimes in their early twenties—in the Amish community are given the opportunity to act out without being shunned by the rest of the group. Some of them leave the places where they grew up and travel to the big city so they can experience what the outside world is like. I was on my own version of a *rumspringa* when I came to Las Vegas and met your father."

"Why here?" I asked, genuinely curious. I loved my hometown, but I knew it wasn't exactly what you could call a huge tourist destination.

"Well, Las Vegas was supposed to be just a stop for me," she admitted. "I was on my way to Albuquerque, and from there to Phoenix and L.A. eventually, or maybe San Francisco. It was well past lunch and I was getting hungry and needed gas, so I pulled off the highway and came into town, and ended up at Charlie's. That's where I met your father—he'd also come there to grab a bite."

Something I'd never known. My father hadn't

wanted to talk about how he met my mother, so after a few early attempts of mine had gotten rudely rebuffed, I hadn't bothered to ask again. In my mind, I'd imagined some kind of fated encounter where their eyes met across a crowded room and the rest was history, but it seemed reality had turned out to be a lot more prosaic than that.

Maybe I nodded. Alicia appeared to take that as a signal to continue, so she went on, "We started talking, and then he said he needed to get back to work but that he'd like to take me out to dinner that night. We ended up going back to Charlie's—neither the Plaza nor the Castañeda had been remodeled and reopened back then, and there was no Skillet, either. But that didn't matter. I just knew by the end of the meal that I was in love...or at least, I thought I was."

Head over heels for a guy she'd only just met. Some people might have considered such impetuousness romantic, but I thought the way she'd fallen for my father only showed a massive lack of judgment...and self-control.

"And that was the end of your *rumspringa?*" I asked.

Her shoulders lifted. "Sort of," she replied. "That is, I really thought I could settle down here, but I started to go stir crazy after a few months. By then I was already pregnant with you, so it wasn't as though I could just pick up and leave."

I had to ask the question, even if I wasn't sure whether I really wanted to hear the answer. "What did your family think about all of this?"

"They told me I could do as I pleased, but because I'd married someone without their permission, they wouldn't offer any support to me...or the child I was carrying." Her eyes met mine across the table, pleading. "I know it sounds old-fashioned, but that's how it works in my family. Magic is passed from generation to generation, but only in the women. And because we have to be so careful about hiding our talents from others, the family chooses who we can marry, someone who can be entrusted with our secrets."

It all sounded crazy to me, but I'd be the first to admit that families could be kind of nuts about a lot of things. But....

"If the Petrucci talent only passes through the female line," I said, "I'm surprised they didn't tell you to bring me with you. I'd think a girl baby would be important to them."

Alicia didn't blink. "Oh, they would have made me take you back to New York...if they'd known," she replied. "But I told them I had a boy, and they didn't care about that. It's why I had to leave you behind—I had to make sure your life would be your own."

For a second or two, I could only stare back at

her. On the surface, her story made some sense, but....

"This isn't a hundred years ago," I told her. "They could have had plenty of ways to find out I was really a girl. There's something called the internet, you know."

Just as Alicia was about to reply, the waiter reappeared with our entrées. I really didn't have much of an appetite by that point, but I still thanked him as he set the plate down in front of me, then shook my head when he asked if there was anything else I needed.

"It didn't occur to them that I might have lied," she said. "I'd been utterly truthful about everything else, so they didn't see the need to investigate. Besides, I went back to New York like a dutiful daughter, married the man they wanted me to marry, had another daughter and a son."

Wait a second....

"You mean I have a *brother and sister?*" I demanded. My head was spinning, and I knew it wasn't because of the few sips of wine I'd allowed myself so far. "Why didn't you tell me?"

"I wasn't sure if I wanted to," she responded. She'd picked up a fork but had yet to dive into her plate of ravioli. "I knew you'd want to meet them, and that's impossible."

Voice tight, I said, "'Impossible' how?"

"You're safe here because everyone in my family

thinks you're male," Alicia said calmly. "If the elder Petrucci witches who run things find out you're a young woman, they'll come and get you, make you come to New York and live by their rules...*all* their rules, including making sure they find someone they consider a suitable husband for you. Do you honestly want that?"

No, of course I didn't. Northern New Mexico suited me just fine, and besides, there was no way in the world I'd put up with strangers telling me who I could or couldn't marry. And even though I still had a lot to learn about the magic from that side of the family, I had to believe the witches who were running things over there must be insanely powerful. Voice flat, I said, "So...I stay here and keep my head down, and everything stays the way it is?"

"Basically."

"And your husband is all right with you driving all over the country by yourself?" I inquired next, thinking her behavior seemed strange for someone whose family was so controlling. "He didn't ask why you were coming to New Mexico in the middle of winter?"

"He can't ask me anything—he passed away three months ago," she said, her tone now almost brittle, as though my innocent question had brought up a host of feelings she'd been doing her best to ignore. She added, "He was quite a bit older than I."

How much older, I probably didn't want to know. At any rate, I thought I could piece together the puzzle now—her husband was gone, and she'd done her duty by her family by having children with him. Now she just wanted to know what had happened to the infant girl she'd left behind all those years ago.

"Anyway," she went on, "I needed to see you, but I wasn't free to come here in person until after my husband was gone. I did do my best to keep track of you over the years, just to make sure you were doing all right. When you started doing the tea-leaf readings, I realized you'd inherited the gift of the Sight from your father's side of the family, and I wanted to come here and find out for myself whether you'd also gotten the Petrucci magic."

"I thought you said it passes from mother to daughter," I pointed out.

"It does," she replied calmly. "But sometimes the gifts are strong, and sometimes they're so weak that their only real value is in being carried over to the next generation in the hope that they'll be stronger next time. That was why I needed to see you in person...and to show you how to work with those talents in case you'd inherited enough of them to be useful."

I didn't know about "useful," but my magic

was definitely pretty strong. "And now that you know...." I said, and let the words trail off.

She finally cut a ravioli in half and speared a piece of it with her fork. After she chewed and swallowed, she said, "Now that I know—and now that your police chief has dropped those ridiculous charges against me—I can go back to New York, and you can go on with your life. I took a risk coming here, one I won't take again. When I left, I told my children that I needed some time to be alone and clear my head, and since they thought I was still grieving their father, they didn't argue. But if I keep coming back to Las Vegas, they're going to suspect something."

If the lives of the Petrucci women were as constrained by their elders as Alicia made it sound, then yes, her kids would definitely begin to wonder why their mother had suddenly taken it in her head to get in her car and drive aimlessly around the country. Obviously, she wouldn't tell them the truth about where she was going—it seemed pretty clear to me that Alicia Petrucci was just fine with spreading a few lies around if they served her purposes—but I had to believe her family would start digging if she made herself scarce too often.

And if that happened, it wouldn't take long for them to follow the trail to Las Vegas...and to a woman there who looked uncannily like their mother.

While one part of me was relieved to finally hear the truth, I couldn't quite ignore the anger churning away inside. So many lies...told both to me and my father, and to her own family. It seemed pretty clear that Alicia's impulse control was sorely lacking, and we'd all suffered for it.

Except her, it seemed. Now that she'd unburdened herself, she looked almost relaxed, ready to dig into the plate of ravioli in front of her. She picked up the second half of the ravioli she'd cut into and put it in her mouth, then speared another one with her fork, obviously ready to get the assembly line going.

As for myself, I wasn't sure whether I'd be able to eat a single bite, even though the chicken plate in front of me smelled absolutely heavenly. However, I didn't want to show Alicia how much she'd upset me, so I resolutely picked up my knife and fork and cut a slice from the breast, then put it in my mouth.

I supposed it tasted good. Right then, I was more focused on making sure it went down and stayed down.

An uneasy silence hovered over the table as we both ate. Then Alicia said, "You're upset."

No point in denying it, although I wasn't going to come right out and tell her what I was feeling.

She hadn't earned the right to know what was in my heart.

"It's a lot to take in," I said after an uncomfortable pause.

"I know," she said. "If I could have come sooner, I would. But until Henry passed away...."

Once again, her words trailed off, drifting into the ether, as though she'd stopped herself when she'd realized how bad it would sound to confess that her life hadn't been her own until she was widowed.

I honestly didn't know what I would have done if I'd been in her shoes, so I just said, "It's okay."

It wasn't, and I had a feeling she knew that. But at least she didn't try to protest, or ask any probing questions. No, I could tell she only wanted to get this over with.

And I was all too happy to oblige her. Neither one of us said anything much after that, except to comment on the food. When the check came, I didn't even try to pick it up. Alicia could afford to pay for the meal, and while I didn't like the idea of being beholden to her in any way, I also didn't see the point in trying to pretend that I had more disposable income than she did.

After she'd signed the check and returned her credit card to her purse, the two of us rose from our chairs and put on our coats, then headed out into the freezing night. The clouds from earlier in the day had finally disappeared, and the sky overhead was coal black, studded with diamond-bright stars.

Alicia walked me to my car, and again, I didn't protest. I could tell she wanted to make these little gestures in an attempt to atone for her neglect over the past couple of decades, and even though I knew none of it would make any difference, I wasn't going to disabuse her of the notion.

No, I just wanted to go home and go to bed, and figure out how to feel about Alicia Petrucci much later, after she'd put a safe distance between the two of us.

"Take care of yourself, Skye," she said.

"I will," I replied, then unlocked the car door. "You have a safe drive back to New York."

She only nodded, and after I got inside my Subaru and closed the door behind me, she slowly walked away, heading toward her white BMW, which was parked a few spots down from my car.

After she climbed in and shut the door, I went ahead and backed out of my parking space.

I knew I'd never see her again.

CHAPTER 13

Family Feud

T he Castañeda Hotel was located less than a
mile from my house, but the drive home
still felt interminable. I supposed I should have
been happy that the weather had cleared up and I
didn't have to worry about dodging snowflakes all
the way back, and yet right then, I didn't think I
could feel very happy about much of anything.

She'd lied. There was no prophecy. There was
nothing particularly special about me.

Okay, some people would probably have
argued that being able to make a cat talk or having
the ability to flit around the ground floor of my
house like an overgrown moth wasn't exactly the
kind of stuff most ordinary people could do, but
still. It seemed like I was a run-of-the-mill Petrucci,
stronger than most, but I definitely wasn't the
chosen one or anything like that.

Which was just fine by me. I'd never had a messiah complex and was completely content to live a quiet, normal life. No, what really bothered me was the way Alicia had lied in order to make herself look a little better.

She told you the truth in the end, I thought as I got out of the car and hurried up the back steps. *That should count for something...especially since that confession made her look even worse than if she'd told you the ugly truth from the very beginning.*

Maybe so. At the moment, I wasn't feeling very charitable. Had she uttered that first lie in order to set me up in case it turned out my gifts didn't amount to much? *Oh, sorry, kid guess you weren't the chosen one after all. Gotta go.*

Considering how she didn't seem to worry too much about the feelings of others, I could see that scenario making some sense. And then when she'd realized my magic had bred true after all, she had to find a way to extricate herself from the lie she'd told me, and providing the truth had turned out to be the easiest way for her to feel as though she'd done the right thing.

No matter what else was going on, it didn't feel too good to realize my mother came across as a borderline sociopath.

Just as I put the key in the lock to the back door, my phone rang from inside my purse. While my first impulse was to immediately pull it out—I didn't get many phone calls in the evening, so I figured it must be important—I also didn't want to stand on the back stoop in the frigid air while I took the call.

So I turned the key and hurried into the house, and then put my purse down on the kitchen table so I could scrabble around inside and find my phone.

Max.

"Hey, what's up?" I said, hoping I didn't sound too breathless from my quick scurry to get inside.

"I'm not calling too late, am I?"

A quick glance at the clock on the stove told me it was just a little past eight. Yes, I went to bed early because of having to be at Levitation Latte at five-thirty in the morning, but even I didn't go to sleep before nine.

"No," I replied. "I'm just getting back from having dinner with Alicia."

"How'd it go?"

I let myself grimace because I knew Max couldn't see my face. "Not great. She's actually going back to New York tomorrow, since the charges against her were dropped."

"Oh."

Just a single syllable, but I'd known him long enough that I understood the brief reply still held a world of meaning. He obviously didn't approve of her skipping town the moment her name was cleared, even if he wasn't going to come right out and say it to my face.

Not that I would have taken offense, since I'd been thinking pretty much the same thing.

"Anyway," he went on, his tone becoming brisker and much more cheerful, "I was wondering if you had any plans tomorrow night."

"On Valentine's Day?" I blurted, then wished I'd held back the question, or at least hadn't sounded so startled.

"Yeah, it's Valentine's Day," he replied, sounding completely unperturbed by that prospect. "And it feels weird to be sitting home alone, even if it is kind of a manufactured holiday. And since I know you're not seeing anybody—"

I tried not to wince, because I could tell Max's invitation was coming from a good place, even if he might not have had all the evidence in hand. "Not formally," I said, hoping I sounded breezy and off-hand. "But I actually have dinner plans with Justin Hale from the *Fix My Town* team on Wednesday night."

A brief silence followed that announcement. I couldn't tell whether Max was startled that I had a date coming up this week, or whether he was trying to figure out if Justin had purposely avoided taking me out on Valentine's Day so as not to give the wrong impression.

"Well, that's Wednesday," Max said reasonably.

"But there's no reason you can't come over tomorrow night, is there? Lou said he'd make us some pizza."

Lou was one of Max's bodyguards...and also a total genius in the kitchen. It had been way too long since I'd had one of Lou's pizzas, so I sure as heck wasn't going to turn it down now.

"That sounds awesome," I replied. "What time?"

"Six-thirty?"

I knew that was probably earlier than Max would have liked to eat dinner, and was dialing in the time to accommodate me.

"Perfect," I said. "Should I bring anything?"

"No, just yourself. I got a fun-looking montepulciano the last time I was in Santa Fe, so I figured we could try that."

Because I'd known he wouldn't want me to supply the wine, I'd asked the question more out of habit than anything else. He had much more free time to drive to Santa Fe or even Albuquerque when the mood took him, so I'd already guessed he had something much more interesting in his wine rack than anything I could've gotten locally.

"Okay, six-thirty tomorrow," I said. "See you then."

We ended the call, and I put the phone back in my purse, then decided to head out to the living room so I could put my feet up and watch some TV until it was time to go to bed.

As I went, I found myself smiling. Yes, dinner with Alicia had been pretty much a disaster, but soon enough she'd be out of my life forever. That call from Max had reminded me I really did have a life here...and people who cared about me.

Alicia could keep the Petruccis and their magic. I wasn't going to say that I would never use my own magic ever again, but I really didn't need it.

I was just fine on my own.

The next morning, Deanne was full of questions about what had happened at my dinner with Alicia. I gave her a compressed version, but even that was enough to make her pink-glossed mouth turn down in disapproval.

"You're better off without her," my friend announced when I was done with my recitation, and I nodded.

"I know," I said. "So I'm doing my best not to worry about it. In a way, it's kind of good to know she won't be popping back into my life whenever she feels like it."

At least, that was the conclusion I'd come to the night before as I lay awake and stared up at the ceiling, praying that sleep would come soon. Most of the time, I was asleep as soon as I turned out the light, but those unsettling revelations from Alicia had been enough to keep my thoughts churning way later than I would have liked.

And yet, knowing she was gone—or would be soon—had lifted a weight from my shoulders I hadn't even realized I was carrying until after it disappeared. It had been harder than I'd thought it would be to try to figure out how to accept her into my life, how to forgive her for what she'd done to me and my father.

Now, though, I didn't need to worry about forgiveness. Maybe one day I'd get to that place... although it seemed as though I had more to forgive her for now than ever before...but for the moment, it was just good to know that things were going to get back to normal.

Wanting to change the subject, I asked, "Did you hear anything about the guy they arrested in here yesterday?"

Deanne shook her head. "Not really," she replied, her expression telling me she wasn't too thrilled about the total lack of information on the subject. "I mentioned it to Mike last night at dinner, but all he'd heard was that someone was in jail for Jessica Rosenthal's murder. I guess the deputies don't have much opportunity to drop by his department and chat."

No, probably not. It made much more sense

for Kyle to come by the coffee shop, even though he'd definitely made himself scarce the day before. Had Las Vegas really been that full of speeding motorists and burglars that particular Monday, or had he purposely been avoiding me so I couldn't ask any probing questions?

He'd definitely never been reticent about sharing police business before, but maybe Chief DeVargas had found out about the way he tended to hang out at Levitation Latte and gossip with Deanne and me, and had put the kibosh on that behavior.

It would stink if that was really what had happened, but I told myself not to borrow trouble. There could be a perfectly reasonable explanation as to why he hadn't dropped by the past couple of days.

In the meantime, the two of us had a shop to get ready to open in the next hour. And although I'd been just about to open my mouth and let Deanne know about my dinner with Max tonight, I decided to stay quiet on the subject. Better to tell her about it after it was a *fait accompli,* even though I doubted there would be much tea to spill on that particular subject. Once again, he'd made it pretty clear that this was simply a friends dinner and nothing more.

But Deanne probably would have wanted to make more out of it than it really was, so I stayed quiet. I knew she had dinner plans with Mike to go to the restaurant at the Plaza Hotel; for really special occasions, he usually took her out to eat in Santa Fe, but Valentine's fell on a work night this year, and that meant they were staying closer to home.

Every time the door opened, I craned my head, hoping each newcomer might be Kyle, but it looked like he didn't plan to make an appearance today, either.

Or maybe he had the day off. His schedule tended to change from week to week, since Chief DeVargas wanted to make sure that none of her deputies were stuck always working nights and weekends, and I'd long ago stopped trying to keep track of who was on duty when.

I tried to tell myself that it wasn't a big deal, that they had a suspect in custody and Alicia was off the hook, so there really wasn't any reason for me to be involved in the case from now on.

But I still had an odd little feeling in my gut that Elliott Rosenthal wasn't the killer any more than my mother had been. I didn't know why my instincts were telling me the police had the wrong man, except there'd been something about his expression as he stood across the room from where Deanne and I had been watching the incident go down, a certain resignation that seemed to signal he knew why the police had zeroed in on him...even as he also knew they were dead wrong. And after seeing what Max had gone through when he was wrongly accused of murder, I hated to see that very same thing happen to another innocent man.

A sudden thought hit me, and I turned to Deanne, asking, "Do you mind watching the store for a while? I need to go out."

Since I very rarely abandoned her to manage the shop for me unless I had a doctor's appointment or something, she sent me a curious look. "To do what?"

"I want to talk to the guy they arrested yesterday."

At once, her expression brightened. "Ooh, did you see something in your tea leaves?"

"Not really," I replied. There didn't seem to be much point in mentioning the hand shape that had been left behind on the side of the teacup, since it didn't seem to mean much of anything. "Just a feeling. And because I don't really have any other leads right now, I thought I might as well try to talk to him."

"Do you think they'll let you?" Deanne asked, now looking dubious.

Good question. I wasn't sure how all this worked, but then again, it wasn't like the guy was on death row.

Yet.

"Well, if they don't, I'll have had a nice walk

across the plaza," I told her. "But even if they let me in to see him, this shouldn't take very long."

"Take as long as you want," she said. "You know it'll be pretty dead from now until closing."

True enough. We were past both the morning and lunch rushes, and even though people might still come in to get an afternoon latte or a muffin to keep them going until dinner, it shouldn't be so many that Deanne would be overwhelmed. Besides, since it was Valentine's Day, people were more interested in buying cakes and cookies and fancy pastries at this point in the afternoon, something they could take home for dessert, and not a croissant or a blueberry muffin.

I thanked her, then went into the back of the shop so I could put on my coat and scarf. No point in getting out my hat, since the day was sunny if cold, and I wasn't going very far.

Quite a few people were out walking their dogs in the park, despite the chilly temperatures, and I smiled at them as I went. If anyone was wondering why Skye O'Malley was out and about at two in the afternoon instead of manning the counter at Levitation Latte, no one stopped me to ask any questions.

Thank God.

Darcy Montoya was working at the front desk when I came in. She shot me a curious glance, mostly because, while she knew that Kyle and I had once dated, she also knew that relationship had been over for almost a year. I guessed she must be wondering why I'd come in, especially since I'd already popped in the day before to drop off some of the cookies I'd baked over the weekend.

Well, she was about to find out why I'd come to the station two days in a row.

"You're holding a man named Elliott Rosenthal, right?" I said, and Darcy nodded, looking even more confused.

"Yes—his bail hearing is set for tomorrow morning."

"Can I talk to him?"

Now her nose wrinkled in continuing confusion. "What for?"

"He was arrested at my shop yesterday," I replied. "I wanted to ask him why he came in there if he knew the police were after him."

Her brows drew together, and I got the feeling she wasn't entirely convinced by my reply. "Well...."

"Is he not allowed visitors?" I asked, and Darcy shook her head.

"I guess he is," she said. "I mean, he's been charged but bail hasn't been set, and he's allowed thirty minutes per visitor per week while he's being held here. So...I guess it's okay?"

That last sentence ended on an upward inflection, as if she was asking me for permission. Most likely, she'd never encountered this particular situation before. People who wanted to visit a prisoner were usually family members or attorneys. To have me asking to see Mr. Rosenthal when I didn't even know him must have sounded kind of strange.

But then Darcy let out a breath, and she continued, "Just don't stay longer than thirty minutes tops, all right? Chief DeVargas is in Santa Fe for a conference today, so it's not like she's here to say no, but...."

"Half an hour is fine," I said hastily. "I doubt I'll even need that long."

My comment seemed to have the desired effect, because Darcy smiled and replied, "Let me take you back to his cell."

His cell. I got a sudden flash of that awful underground prison row where Hannibal Lecter had been confined in *Silence of the Lambs,* and then told myself not to be silly. This was the Las Vegas police department we were talking about, not some moldering mental facility on the East Coast. And while I knew that the building had a room where prisoners could meet with their attorneys, I guessed Darcy didn't want to take the chance of removing Elliott Rosenthal from his cell.

The jail section of the building was located at the back and consisted of eight cells, none of which were going to win any design awards, although everything looked clean enough. The first cell was occupied by a man who looked like he might be sleeping off a drunk, or maybe a bad fentanyl trip. He lay on his back, eyes shut and face slack, and a snore that felt like it should rattle the bars of his cell escaped from his lips.

The rest of the cells were unoccupied, though... all except the last one.

Elliott Rosenthal sat on his bunk and appeared to be staring off into the middle distance at nothing in particular. He wore an orange jumpsuit and his chin was covered in dark stubble, but otherwise, he didn't look too worse for wear after spending twenty-four hours in a jail cell.

His dark eyes sharpened as he caught sight of me, but he didn't say anything, only sat there in silence as Darcy said, "This is Skye O'Malley. She wants to talk to you for a couple of minutes." In an undertone, she added, "Just come back up front when you're done."

"I will," I said quietly.

She offered me a brief, encouraging smile before heading back the way we'd come. Once she was gone, Elliott said, "You're the girl from the coffee shop."

"I am," I replied. I didn't think I was particularly memorable, but maybe every last detail from the moment when he'd been arrested had been burned into his brain.

"What do you want?"

"The truth," I said.

His mouth twitched a little. "I told the police the truth, but they didn't want to hear it. Why's it so important to you, anyway?"

"Because I don't think you're guilty," I told him.

He didn't even blink. Voice steady, he asked, "What makes you say that?"

"Just a gut feeling."

Now he smiled for real, and reached up a hand to run it through his hair. It was thick and just slightly wavy, the kind of hair that actually looked better messed up a little. And no, he definitely wasn't my type, but I could see why someone like Jessica Rosenthal might have found him attractive.

Of course, his next words shot down that particular theory.

"My sister wasn't much of one for gut feelings."

I stared at him for a second or two before the meaning of his comment began to sink in. "Jessica was your sister?"

"Yes," he said. "My little sister."

"So why...?" I stopped myself there, not sure how I should frame the question.

"Why do the police think I killed her?"

I nodded.

Elliott went back to his bunk and sat down, then let out a breath that wasn't exactly a sigh. "Jessica and I owned a valuable piece of property together. It was left to us by our grandparents—a house on a big lot up in the Hollywood Hills. The house is pretty much a tear-down, but the land is worth millions. We had a buyer, but Jessica kept stringing him along, trying to get him to raise the price. He actually did—on two separate occasions—but after the second time, he told me he was going to move on unless we closed the deal in the next two weeks."

"So you came to Las Vegas, where Jessica was working on her show," I said.

A nod, and Elliott said, "I told her she was going to lose us a big chunk of money if she didn't get her act together. She laughed at me and said we'd have another buyer soon enough, one who was willing to pay even more." A pained expression crossed his face as he added, "I'll admit I lost my temper and yelled at her, and that we continued our argument even as she followed me back to my car. I have a feeling some of the neighbors overheard us, and when the police started investigating her death, they figured I was a natural suspect."

It sure looked that way. Money could make people do horrible things, and I had no doubt that once Chief DeVargas started putting two and two together, she figured it was only logical that Jessica Rosenthal's brother had killed her so he could sell the property in question...and be the sole beneficiary of the sale.

"But you didn't do it," I said.

"Nope," Elliott replied, and rubbed a hand over the stubble on his chin. He looked almost surprised by its presence, as though he hadn't expected it to grow in so quickly. "I wasn't anywhere near the place when she was killed."

"Where were you?" I asked, hoping maybe he had a cast-iron alibi that Chief DeVargas had decided to ignore in favor of a quick conviction.

That sort of behavior didn't sound very much like her, but maybe she was starting to feel desperate after the town's previous two murders had been solved by a rank amateur, namely me.

Elliott grimaced. "In my hotel room at the Best Western. I was watching TV, so it's not as though there are any phone records or emails or logins to prove I was there and not over at Jessica's Airbnb."

Darn it. So much for that alibi.

"Any physical evidence that you were at the scene of the crime?" I asked. Most likely, there must have been or Elliott wouldn't be sitting in this jail cell, but I figured I needed to ask.

Another one of those twists of his mouth. "Fingerprints on the door and other things around the rental. You know, on a glass of water, the Kleenex dispenser in the bathroom. I'd been there a couple of times before things got nasty, so there's plenty of stuff I touched while I was in the house. I tried to explain all that to your police chief, but she didn't want to hear it."

No, Marie DeVargas probably thought she had sufficient evidence for the case to go to trial, so I doubted she would've backed down.

On the surface, it all sounded pretty grim. I couldn't think of anything that might help to prove Elliott Rosenthal's innocence...unless something miraculous happened and I was able to figure out the identity of the real killer.

"I'm sorry about your sister," I said then, thinking it had to be extra hard to be wrongly accused of killing someone and then not even being allowed to grieve properly.

He didn't quite shrug, but I got the feeling he wasn't quite as affected by Jessica's death as I'd thought he might be.

"She was kind of a hard-ass," he said, tone almost dismissive. "We never got along very well, although mostly we just ignored each other and went on with our lives. I didn't like getting in her face over this real estate deal because I knew what a pain she was to deal with, but I also wasn't going to let her lose us millions of dollars."

No, that was definitely the sort of thing to make a person impatient, even angry.

Angry enough to kill?

I still didn't think so.

But since I didn't have much else to ask—or

anything I could do to get him out of here—I only said, "Well, thank you for talking to me. I don't know if any of this will help, but you've given me a lot to think about."

"Any time," Elliott said, and then shot a grimly amused glance at his drab surroundings. "It's not like I'm going anywhere."

About all I could do was shake my head. Even though I knew I probably had a good bit of time left in my allotted half hour, I couldn't think of anything else to ask him. Instead, I thanked him again and headed out, thoughts churning away.

Could my instincts be completely off base on this? Could Elliott Rosenthal really be the killer? He definitely had motive, and opportunity. After all, even if they were at odds, Jessica would have opened her door to him, let him inside her rented house. The details were still sketchy, but from what I'd heard so far, there didn't seem to have been any sign of forced entry.

Meaning that she'd known her killer?

Maybe.

I let out a sigh as I emerged into the frosty air, that puff of breath visible for a second or two before the water vapor it contained evaporated.

Elliott had given me some valuable information...but I still didn't know what to do with it.

CHAPTER 14

King of Hearts

When I got back to the coffee shop, I filled Deanne in on what Elliott Rosenthal had just told me. She pursed her lips and said, "That doesn't sound very good."

"No, it doesn't," I agreed. "But even though he seems like a logical suspect, I really don't think he killed his sister."

For a moment, my friend was silent. While she tended to agree with my instincts about people, in this particular case, I got the feeling she thought I was grasping at straws.

Maybe so. But, while I didn't know Elliott Rosenthal very well, I had to believe if he'd come to Las Vegas with murder in his heart, he wouldn't have made quite such a public display of his beef with his sister, letting the whole neighborhood where her Airbnb was located hear him have it out with her about that expensive piece of real estate in the Hollywood Hills. No, he would have played nice until he had the opportunity to strike.

We had a late afternoon rush of high school kids picking up mochaccinos and muffins on their way home, so Deanne and I didn't have much opportunity to talk after that. And while being busy until the very last minute could sometimes be tiring, I had to admit it was nice to have the bakery case completely cleaned out so there wasn't anything that needed to be taken home or walked over to the deputies at the police station, who were often the beneficiary of any leftovers we might have on hand.

She was excited to get ready for her Valentine's Day dinner with Mike, and I played along, not letting on that I had my own plans for that evening. And no, I didn't get all dressed up, only changed into something that was clean and stylish without being an obvious date-night outfit.

Because this wasn't a date. This was just a couple of friends getting together for a kind of lonely-hearts dinner, since we were both currently unattached.

I wanted to smile at that admittedly naïve view of the situation. If he'd wanted to, Max could have crooked a finger and had all sorts of women come running to be at his side, even if doing so would mean spending time in a podunk town like Las Vegas, New Mexico.

While I...well, let's just say the list of people willing to drop everything to be with me was a *lot* shorter.

Not completely empty, though. I had my dinner with Justin to look forward to, and no doubt Kyle would have been happy to spend this Valentine's Day with me if I'd asked. No, I hadn't seen him since he'd come into the shop to arrest Elliott Rosenthal, but I still had his information on my contacts list. Maybe I should have deleted it, although, considering he was one of my best suppliers of information about crime in the town, doing something like that would have been kind of stupid.

It was full dark by the time I left the house. Not that it mattered much, because I'd driven back and forth from Max's ranch so many times, I probably could have made the journey blindfolded.

Al Torres, Max's other security guard, was on duty at the gate when I drove up. This didn't surprise me too much, since I guessed Lou must be inside putting the final touches on our pizza for the evening.

I waved at Al, and he waved back and smiled at me before I headed through the gate. It was dark out there, true, but he had a camping lantern next to him, along with a barrel full of logs he was burning to keep warm. Even with that extra bit of creature comfort—and seeing that he was bundled up in a puffer coat, wool cap, muffler, and gloves—I couldn't help thinking it had to be pretty uncomfortable to stand out there for any length of time. Couldn't Max rely on a security camera when the weather was this cold? I had a hard time believing even the most intrepid paparazzo...especially one used to Southern California's much balmier weather...would want to be lurking out here in the chill of a February evening.

But when I tried to comment on the way he was perched out here by himself, Al only chuckled. "I like the cold. Keeps me on my toes. Max tried to tell me to come inside, but I'm fine out here for now. You go on, and have a good evening."

So I'd kept driving, and when I arrived at the house, all was warmth and light. Pretty fixtures with flickering Edison-style bulbs flanked the front door, and the friendly scent of wood smoke drifted on the night air, telling me Max must have stoked up the fireplace.

When he opened the door, the aroma got stronger, along with something so savory and enticing, my stomach wanted to growl in response.

"Come on in," Max told me, stepping aside so I could enter the foyer. "Let me get your coat." I unzipped my puffer jacket and handed it over, along with my scarf and hat. He stowed all those items in the hall closet, then said, "Let's head into the dining room."

I sniffed the air, trying to identify that amazing aroma. "I thought Lou was making us pizza."

"He is," Max replied. "But this was something new he wanted to try—mushrooms sautéed in marsala wine and butter. Smells great, doesn't it?"

"More than great," I said. I knew some people didn't care for mushrooms, but I wasn't in that club. "You know I love mushrooms."

"That's what I told Lou when he was figuring out what kind of pizza to make."

By then we'd entered the dining room, where the big table had two place settings at one end, and where the bottle of montepulciano Max had mentioned earlier sat at the head of the table, already opened and starting to air.

"Where is Lou, anyway?" I asked, glancing around.

"Oh, he took off once he was done with the pizza," Max said. "It's keeping warm in the oven. You go ahead and sit down, and I'll get it."

Because Lou often seemed to leave the scene once he was done cooking, I wouldn't allow myself to assign any ulterior motives to his absence now. Otherwise, I might have thought he'd purposely left so Max and I could share a romantic dinner without worrying about being interrupted.

A moment later, he returned with the pizza laid

out on a big wooden peel. Up close like this, it smelled even more delectable.

"You should've had Lou approach the *Fix My Town* people," I remarked as Max used a mezzaluna to cut the pizza into neat slices. "One bite of his pizza, and they would've funded a new restaurant for him."

Max grinned as he slid a slice onto my plate, then did the same for himself. With us both settled for the moment, he sat down in the chair at the head of the table and responded, "He wouldn't need to go to them for funding. I've already told him I'd be happy to give him the seed money to open a restaurant."

"And what did he say to that?" I asked, forcing myself to wait while Max poured us both some wine.

"He said he was happy just cooking for me and Al, but if he ever got bitten by the restaurant bug, he'd let me know." Max raised his glass. "Happy Valentine's Day."

I touched my glass to his and echoed the words, even if I wasn't sure whether I really meant them or not. Yes, it was great to be here with him—much better than sitting at home and feeling sorry for myself—but there wasn't anything remotely romantic about this dinner. He hadn't lit the candles on the table, and the fixture overhead had been dimmed only slightly, not enough to create anything close to mood lighting.

"How's the murder investigation going?" he asked after we'd both drunk some wine and helped ourselves to one of the pieces of pizza he'd cut a moment earlier.

My mouth twisted. "Not great. I actually got to talk to Elliott Rosenthal—you know, the guy who was arrested at my shop yesterday—for a couple of minutes, but I'm not sure how much it helped. I mean, I can see why the police might think he was guilty, but I just don't believe it."

"Why's that?"

So I launched into a brief recap of my conversation with Mr. Rosenthal, explaining how Jessica had been dragging her heels on a profitable real estate deal, and that was why Elliott had come to Las Vegas in the first place.

"But he's right," I concluded. "If he really had come here with the intent to kill her, then he wouldn't have been so openly vocal about the way she was handling the real estate deal. I just think he was at the wrong place at the wrong time."

Max nodded, then took a bite of pizza. "And Alicia?"

I couldn't help noticing the way he'd carefully referred to her by her first name and not as "your mother." Fine by me—I was going to work really hard not to think of her that way, either.

"Oh, she's off the hook and gone back to New York."

His expression shifted, now showing only concern. "How do you feel about that?"

From somewhere, I dredged up a dreary smile. "Ask me again in a couple of years."

He wisely took the hint and moved the conversation to safer topics, like the work being done around Las Vegas, including the gorgeous metal sign Ben Fredricks was erecting at the south end of town. Justin had mentioned the metal sculptor's name, but with everything else that had been going on, it had completely slipped my mind that my hometown's makeover was including more than the two projects downtown and the renovation at Pastor Phil's house.

"It's definitely going to be a different Las Vegas when they're done," I agreed, and took another bite of pizza before washing it down with some more wine. The pizza tasted even better than it smelled, and, while my first impulse was to ask Max if he could get the recipe from Lou, I decided against it. Sometimes it was nice to let people cook for you...especially if you weren't sure you'd be able to perfectly replicate their efforts.

Max leaned back in his chair. "Hopefully, that's a good thing. I kind of like it the way it is."

"With a busted movie theater that looks like

something out of 1972 and limited dining options?"

The question made him grin, as I'd hoped it would. "Well, all right...I'll admit the theater could use some work. And I'm willing to see what Bruce and Skyler do with the old cowboy emporium. But still, I don't want Las Vegas changed too much. There's a reason why I decided to come back here, and it wasn't because I thought the town needed an overhaul."

While I would have liked to ask exactly what that reason was, I remained silent. There wasn't any point in fooling myself that my presence here had been any kind of an incentive.

No, he'd come back to Las Vegas because he was tired of the L.A. rat race and wanted a place where he could have some much-needed peace and quiet, and finding the perfect property in his old hometown where he could be close to his family was only the icing on the cake. Renewing his acquaintance with the girl next door had probably been pretty low on his list.

"Luckily, there's only so much one TV show can do, right?" I said. "It's not like they're going to be changing everything."

"Thank God for that," he replied with another of his movie-marquee smiles, and downed some more wine.

I had to agree with him. And even though I'd

been considering whether I should mention again that I had a date the next evening with one of the *Fix My Town* crew members, I decided to keep quiet on the subject. What would be the point? It would only look like I really was trying to make him jealous. We weren't in high school anymore, and playing games to try to pique his interest had never been my style. Either he'd come to realize we worked well together, or he wouldn't.

If not, well...like I'd said to him earlier when we were talking about Alicia, I'd figure out how I felt about that a few years from now.

No kiss goodnight or anything, although Max did surprise me by giving me a quick hug after he walked me to the door and I slipped into my coat.

"I'm sorry about this whole thing with Alicia," he said, after he'd let me go and I stared at him somewhat dazedly, wondering how I should react. "I know you were hoping you could have some kind of a relationship with her."

"It's okay," I said, an automatic response, not anything I actually meant. Better to focus on what he'd said, and not my reaction to that off-hand embrace. "I'm not really sure what I was expecting. But she taught me how to work with my magic, so that's something positive that came out of meeting her. Anyway, I'm just planning to go on with my life and not worry about her or what she's doing."

For a moment, he looked almost diffident, as if he knew he should say something comforting but couldn't come up with the right words. Then he reached out and squeezed my hand. "You're going to be okay, Skye."

His words carried such conviction that I didn't dare contradict him. No, I only ducked my head and said I hoped so, and then hurried out the door.

As I drove away, I found myself hoping he was right.

* * *

The next morning, though, I realized I was feeling better about life than I maybe had any right to. True, I still hadn't figured out who really had murdered Jessica Rosenthal, and I was still as firmly in the friend zone with Max as I'd ever been.

But the sun was shining brightly, and I'd survived Valentine's Day, although my brain continued to process that hug Max had given me, trying to figure out if there had been anything more to it than reassurance from a friend.

Aside from that, though, tonight I had a date with Justin. Things were looking up, even as I acknowledged to myself that the two of us didn't have much of a future. He'd finish here and move on to the next town the show would focus on, and that would be that.

Again, I reminded myself there wasn't anything wrong with having fun, even if all we might have was a couple of dates. Besides, although I liked him and thought he was cute, I certainly didn't know enough about him to even begin to form an opinion as to our compatibility.

It was a quiet enough day, only broken up by something odd I noticed when I went down the street to buy a packet of pens from Paper Trail—a fun shop a few doors down from Levitation Latte that sold all sorts of interesting stuff but also carried some office supplies—since all of ours apparently decided to die at exactly the same time. Across Bridge Street and down a couple of storefronts, the *Fix My Town* crew was busy at the cowboy emporium, which in and of itself wasn't all that strange.

However, Justin was standing out front and having what looked like some kind of heated discussion with the pretty girl who'd come into the coffee shop a few days earlier, the woman with the long brown hair and big hazel eyes. From where I stood, I couldn't hear what they were saying, but it definitely looked as though they weren't very happy with each other.

Well, based on a few tidbits Max had let drop, I'd gotten the impression that sometimes tempers flared on set, and I supposed it wasn't much different when you were filming a reality TV show instead of a movie. And actually, considering the way I'd wanted to let some of my contractors have it during the remodel of my own house, I thought it might be even more high-pressure when you threw in all the thousand and one things that could go wrong with a renovation and added them to the usual stress of working in the television industry.

Anyway, it wasn't any of my business. Maybe Justin would bring up the squabble at dinner tonight and maybe he wouldn't, but that was his decision. I definitely didn't want to stand there and gawk, so I hurried back up the street to Levitation Latte and did my best to put the incident out of my mind.

Because, whatever was going on down at the cowboy emporium, the lunch rush would be upon us soon, and I needed to focus on that, not reality-show drama.

After lunch, Kyle Isaacs finally made an appearance at the shop. I tried not to show how relieved I was to see him—mostly because I didn't want to give him the wrong idea—but I knew I was a little quicker than usual to pour him a cup of coffee and slide a muffin and its plate across the display case toward him.

"Been busy?" I asked, doing my best to sound casual.

I didn't know whether he bought it or not, but at least his expression didn't change as he lifted his shoulders, then swallowed some coffee.

"I had yesterday off," he said. "So I drove down to Albuquerque to do some shopping."

That didn't sound like a lot of fun, especially considering how iffy the weather had been, but there were a lot of things you just couldn't get in Las Vegas or even Santa Fe. That meant you had to do without, unless you mail-ordered what you needed...or took the time to drive all the way to our state's biggest population center.

"But," Kyle went on before I could respond, "we turned up some new evidence in the Rosenthal case."

"Oh?" I said, even as Deanne sidled closer so she wouldn't miss out on any of the details.

Now Kyle grinned, showing me that he'd seen right through my nonchalant act. "Yeah, it was kind of strange. Jessica Rosenthal had some leather scraps under her fingernails, as if she'd been digging or tearing at something—probably a pair of gloves —before she died."

"Her attacker?" Deanne asked.

"Maybe," Kyle replied. "But her brother's prints were all over the house, so I don't see why he would have bothered to wear gloves when he was killing her. I mean, you'd think he would at least have tried to wipe down the place if he was that set on covering up the evidence."

Yes, one would think...unless you were me and already suspected that someone other than Elliott was the one who'd killed Jessica Rosenthal. In that case, it would make perfect sense for her murderer to have worn gloves as he grabbed that phone charging cord and wrapped it around her neck.

But because I hadn't said anything to Kyle about my suspicions—and it looked as though he didn't know anything about my visit with Elliott at the police station the day before—I decided it was better to keep silent on the subject, beyond making a small murmur of assent at his remark.

Deanne, on the other hand, didn't have any problem plowing in where I feared to tread. "So, does this new piece of evidence mean her brother isn't the killer?"

Kyle had just broken off a piece of muffin and stuck it in his mouth as she asked that question, so he had to finish chewing before he could answer. "I don't think it proves anything one way or another. The chief still thinks there's enough evidence that the D.A. will move forward with a trial."

No, short of somehow finding the real killer and extracting a confession from him, I didn't see how Elliott would be able to avoid going to court. Maybe a jury would decide there wasn't enough evidence to implicate him in the crime, but if he really was innocent, I hated the idea of him having to go through all that.

Unfortunately, I didn't have any proof that he hadn't murdered his sister. Until I managed to find it, he'd stay stuck in jail.

And since I had no idea where to even start looking—the tea leaves hadn't been very clear and I hadn't been visited by any true dreams—I had a feeling his situation wasn't going to change any time soon.

CHAPTER 15

Hand in Glove

E ven though I tried to tell myself this dinner with Justin wasn't that big a deal, I still spent more time getting ready for it than I probably should have. No, I didn't bring out my fancy purple wrap dress, the one that had made even Max do a double take when I wore it to a dinner at his house last autumn, but I fussed with my hair and applied more makeup than I normally would, and wore slim jeans and the cashmere sweater Deanne had given me for my birthday.

The whole time, though, I kept thinking about that exchange I'd seen earlier in the day, the one where Justin and the girl from his show were having a difference of opinion on something.

Actually, if I wanted to be completely truthful, they looked like they were on the verge of a full-blown fight.

The girl and her friend had paid cash for their lattes when they came into the shop, so I hadn't seen a credit card and therefore didn't know her name. However, she was obviously at least five or six years younger than I was, too young to be a producer or director. No, she had to be a production assistant of some kind, someone in the kind of role you wouldn't normally think would have the guts to get in the face of a man who could fire her without a second thought.

"Not my circus, not my monkeys," I murmured to myself as I descended the stairs. It wasn't quite six-thirty, definitely too early to head out for my date, considering my dinner destination was only about five minutes away. But because there wasn't much else I could do to get ready— well, except maybe try futzing with false eyelashes, which I hardly ever wore and which would make me look as though I was trying *way* too hard—I figured I might as well hang out in the living room until it was time to leave.

And, just to reassure myself the magic was still there, I stretched out my hand to the remote where it sat on the coffee table. It immediately rose a few inches into the air, sailed across the room, and landed in my palm, telling me these strange gifts were apparently here to stay, even if Alicia was long gone.

Maybe someday I'd figure out what to do with them besides a few parlor tricks.

In the meantime, though, it was enough to take the remote and turn on the TV so I could watch a bit of the Albuquerque news before it was time to head out.

"…the main suspect in the case, Elliott Rosenthal, posted bail today in the amount of half a million dollars and is currently in Las Vegas awaiting trial," the newscaster said. "Details are still limited, but local sources say that Jessica Rosenthal was murdered over a real estate deal. We'll update this developing story when we have more information."

Mouth twisting, I lifted the remote again and turned off the television. Even that little snippet was enough to remind me that the clock was ticking and I definitely didn't have all the time in the world to track down Jessica's murderer. And where had Elliot gotten half a million dollars for bail? He'd never said anything about what he did for a living, but, going solely on the way he'd talked about the Hollywood Hills real estate deal, it sounded as though he'd needed that money pretty badly.

True, he wouldn't have had to come up with the whole $500K, just ten percent of it, but still, most people I knew didn't have fifty grand floating around in their savings accounts.

But at least it was good to know he was out on bail, and presumably had returned to his room at the Best Western. The newscaster hadn't provided many details, but it sounded to me like the judge wanted him to stick around until the trial.

Which meant I really should have been focusing on the case rather than going out to dinner with Justin.

However, the tea leaves hadn't been super-helpful lately, and my dreams came when they wanted and not at my bidding. As things stood, there really wasn't a whole heck of a lot more I could do.

Then why did I feel so guilty?

You are not cheating on Max, I told myself for the umpteenth time. *Get over it.*

I wasn't very good at that, but I figured I'd better try.

At least enough time had passed that it was now close to seven, meaning I needed to get moving. After putting on my hat and scarf—I stashed my gloves in my purse in case I might need them later—I hurried out the door and down the steps, and got into my car as quickly as I could. No, it wasn't quite as cold as the last few days had been, but I still didn't enjoy standing around in thirty-degree weather.

Because it was a Wednesday night, The Skillet wasn't quite as crowded as it would have been on a

Friday or Saturday. All the same, the street in front of the restaurant had enough cars lining its curb that I had to park around the corner and walk farther than I would have liked.

Well, at least it wasn't snowing.

Even though I was right on time, I spotted Justin sitting at one of the tables along the far wall, telling me he must have gotten here a few minutes early. I sent him a smile and headed over, glad that he'd already snagged a place to sit.

"It's busier than I thought it would be," I said as I sat down, and he nodded.

"Yeah, I figured I'd better get here a little early, since this isn't the kind of place where you can exactly make a reservation."

No, it was not. And while at first I'd thought coming here after our aborted first date was supposed to happen at a much fancier restaurant sounded like kind of a letdown, now I realized this was a much better idea. Grabbing a couple of burgers or some tacos at The Skillet took a lot of the pressure off. We could just be friends hanging out and nothing more.

If that was what he even wanted. To be honest, it was kind of hard to get a read off him as to exactly what he was expecting from me. I wasn't the sort of woman who assumed men would just throw themselves at her feet—well, straight, available men, anyway—but considering Justin was the one who'd asked me out and who'd wanted to reschedule after our first date went down in flames, I suppose I'd thought I would see at least a flicker of admiration in his eyes as I sat down.

Then again, I didn't know him very well. Some guys threw off lots of signals, while others might as well have been written in hieroglyphics for all the clues they sent out.

"What's good here?" Justin asked. "I looked at the menu before I sat down, but I figured I'd get a local's input."

I smiled. At The Skillet, you went up to the counter to order, so there weren't any menus supplied at the table. "It's all good. Just depends on whether you want a burger or some tacos, or maybe a salad."

That last bit I tacked on, just because I realized he might be vegetarian or even vegan, in which case, this probably hadn't been the best choice of dinner venues.

But he shook his head, saying, "A burger sounds good. I could use some extra protein after today."

"Tough one?" I asked, hoping I sounded properly sympathetic...but also wondering if he might open up about what was going on with him and the brown-haired girl he'd been arguing with earlier in the day.

"No more so than usual," he replied, and

rubbed his chin. It didn't look like he'd shaved today, which was fine. I liked guys a little scruffy. "Or at least, I guess it feels like more because I'm having to handle all Jessica's work and mine, too. On top of that, one of our carpenters sprained his shoulder, so I was doing some of his work while he supervised."

"You can do woodwork?" I asked, then wondered if I shouldn't have sounded so surprised.

But he didn't look offended, and instead sent me a rueful grin. "Well, I can pound a nail in, I suppose. Without Stan telling me what to do, I doubt I could even put a birdhouse together. Anyway, we should probably order some food. What would you like?"

I had the menu pretty much memorized, so I didn't even hesitate as I told him I'd like a deluxe burger, no pickles, and a side of fries. "And whatever red wine they've got right now," I added, since The Skillet definitely didn't have a standing wine list and pretty much served whatever they'd gotten a deal on that particular week.

"Got it," Justin said, and rose from the table so he could go stand in line to order. There were three people ahead of him, so I knew it was going to take a little while.

However, I didn't reach into my purse and pull out my phone, figuring it would seem rude to be checking my email or scrolling through Instagram while he had to stand there and wait to put in our order. Instead, I looked around the restaurant, trying to see who was there that night, and what I would do if it was someone I knew and they asked who Justin was.

To my relief, though, I didn't see anyone I recognized. Not that I was embarrassed to be there with him or anything, but having to launch into explanations could get kind of awkward.

About five minutes passed, and Justin made it to the head of the line and placed our order. He came back to our table and said, "They'll bring the drinks over in a couple of minutes."

Since I'd been to The Skillet about a million times and definitely knew the drill by now, I just nodded. "Thanks for standing in line."

"Well, it was my idea to come here, so the least I could do was get the orders in." He looked a little sheepish, adding, "Maybe we should have gone back to the Castañeda."

"No, this is fine," I said quickly. I definitely didn't want him to think that I minded the venue, not when it was one of my favorite places to hang out. "I love the food here."

He shifted in his chair, now looking a little more relaxed. "Yeah, it's pretty good. I came here with the crew a couple of days ago to grab dinner, and I thought the burgers were great."

"How is the filming going?" I asked then, glad of the chance to shift the subject.

Judging by the way his expression brightened, I could tell he was also glad that I didn't have any intention of giving him grief about the restaurant he'd chosen for dinner. "Pretty good," he said. "We've got all the plumbing and electrical roughed in for the new kitchen at the Mackenzies' restaurant, and the new seating for the theater is supposed to be here by the end of the week."

"That's great news," I responded. "Those old seats made it feel as though you were sitting in someone's busted 1973 Buick or something."

My remark made him chuckle, and the conversation moved along smoothly enough after that, as both of us grew more relaxed and less worried about whether we were going to stumble over some subject or another that might turn out to be problematic. He had a beer and I had a glass of wine, and because we were so busy talking and eating, it looked like neither one of us needed to order a second drink.

Which I knew was a good thing. It was always better to stay a little sharp on a first date, no matter how well it might be going.

Eventually, our talk wound down, and Justin said, "Well, we don't want to hog this table all night. Besides, I have to be on set early tomorrow."

"And I need to be at the shop at five-thirty," I told him. "So I totally get it."

We got up from our seats and began wrestling ourselves into our coats and hats. "How chilly is out there?" he asked.

"By now?" I replied. "Probably in the upper twenties."

He didn't quite shudder, but I got the definite impression that he'd be glad to be done with the shoot and back in sunny Southern California. "Better bundle up, then," he said, and reached into the messenger bag he'd brought with him, pulling out a dark blue muffler.

A pair of gloves fell out of the bag as he extricated the scarf. "Oh, I'll get those," I said, and bent down to fetch them, even as he began to protest that he could get the gloves himself. As I picked them up, though, a cold shock went right through me.

The fingers on both gloves looked as though they'd been put through a meat grinder, the dark brown leather shredded and torn.

According to Kyle, Jessica Rosenthal had had some kind of leather buried under her fingernails when they did the autopsy.

And that meant....

Justin must have noticed the way I was staring down at the gloves, because he forced a smile even as he reached to take them from me, and said,

"Yeah, they look like crap, don't they? I didn't pack any work gloves, and I had to use these while I was helping the carpenter the other day. They really got destroyed. I tried looking at Walmart for another pair, but they were all out of my size."

While I sure as hell didn't believe his story about helping the carpenter, I guessed the part about looking for replacement gloves at a local store was probably true. He would've wanted to get rid of the evidence if he could but had been stymied by the way our Walmart never seemed to keep what you needed in stock. I had no idea why he hadn't thrown them out and just braved the cold, but maybe as a California native, or at least someone who'd lived there for years, he couldn't handle our current sub-freezing temperatures the way a native might.

Also, that bit of information about the leather being found under Jessica's nails wasn't exactly common knowledge. There was no way in the world Justin could have known Kyle had spilled the beans on that little detail earlier today, so maybe he would have thought he was safe enough even if anyone noticed the tattered condition of his gloves.

Somehow, I managed to say, "Oh, that stinks. They look like they were nice gloves, too." I paused there, thinking furiously, and then added, "You know, I need to hit the bathroom before I head out. I had a really nice time, though."

A look of puzzlement passed over Justin's face. He was probably wondering why I needed to use the restroom when I lived only five minutes away, but to my relief, he didn't ask any uncomfortable questions, only said, "I had a great time, too. You have a safe drive home."

"I will," I said, and gathered up my purse and headed away from the table and down the short hall nearby where the bathrooms were located. A surreptitious glance over my shoulder told me he was already walking toward the front door, so I hurried the last couple of feet to the women's restrooms, locked myself in a stall, and got out my phone.

My first impulse was to text Max—he'd definitely done a good job of coming to the rescue when Evan Bryant tried to shoot me—but I told myself that plan wasn't very wise. Yes, he was an action star, and yet I thought it was a much better idea to have someone official intervene.

So I scanned down my contacts list, stopped at the one for Kyle Isaacs, and started typing furiously.

I'm pretty sure Justin Hale is the killer. He was wearing gloves tonight that looked as though someone or something had torn them up. He's leaving The Skillet now and is probably headed back to the hotel. I'm going to my car now, so I'm okay. Thanks.

Then I hit Send and hoped I hadn't made a huge mistake.

What if it turned out that Justin's excuse for the shredded gloves was a perfectly valid one?

But no, my gut was telling me now that his gloves were destroyed because Jessica had been tearing at them desperately as he wrapped that phone charging cord around her neck. Exactly what had driven him to commit such a horrible act, I didn't know, although I knew one thing.

There had been a very clear reason why the tea leaves had shown me that image of a puffy-looking hand. It hadn't been a hand at all, but a glove. And I'd been too stupid to recognize the symbol for what it was.

I knew I shouldn't be too hard on myself, since the images tea leaves provided weren't exactly as clear-cut as, say, a sketch artist's portrait of a subject. Still, you'd think some alarm bells would have gone off when Kyle started talking about finding those scraps of leather under Jessica's fingernails.

No response to my text, which both annoyed and bothered me. Shouldn't he have been right on it as soon as such an alarming message popped up on his phone?

I reminded myself it was dinnertime, and even though I guessed Kyle was probably off-duty by now, he most likely didn't feel the need to be staring at his phone's screen the entire time.

Well, whatever he was doing, I couldn't hide here in this bathroom stall forever. I flushed the toilet just in case someone had slipped in to fix her makeup in the mirror over the sink, but the women's restroom was completely empty.

And when I emerged and paused by the wall that shielded the bathrooms from the rest of the restaurant space, I didn't see any sign of Justin.

Thank God. I'd been worried he might have decided to linger, that he'd thought maybe it wasn't kosher to leave his date to fend for herself while he went on his merry way.

No such chivalrous thoughts appeared to have plagued him, though, and so the coast was clear. I couldn't allow myself a sigh of relief, though...not yet, anyway.

As I left the restaurant, I stopped again for just a second to make sure he wasn't lurking somewhere nearby, but no, I didn't see him—or anyone else, for that matter, except a couple of kids who looked like they might be high school seniors just getting out of their car.

All right. Time to go.

I hastened down the steps and hung a right so I could get back to the next street over where my car was parked. Snow still lingered in patches that I guessed were shaded during the day, so here and there I had to slow down and watch my footing, even though I'd made sure to wear rubber-soled boots because of this very eventuality.

But there was my Subaru, partially hidden behind a big silvery SUV, a Tahoe or Suburban. Just as I began to move past it, my keys in hand, Justin Hale came out from between the hulking vehicle and my much smaller Outback, a thin smile on his lips.

He stopped in front of me and said, "You figured it out, didn't you?"

CHAPTER 16

Call the Cavalry

My first instinct was to turn tail and run, but Justin was much taller than I, and I just knew he would catch up with me pretty quickly if I attempted to flee. No, even though an icy chill moved through my body that had absolutely nothing to do with the frigid air that surrounded me, I did my best to sound confused as I said, "Figured what out?"

His smile widened a little. We were on a residential street, but since it was so cold and also past the time most people would be getting home from work, he'd probably realized no one would come out to interrupt us. "Figured out about what really happened with Jessica. What, did the tea leaves tell you?"

Damn...I'd really hoped he'd forgotten about that.

Now Justin's expression—what I could see of it from the illumination provided by a streetlight half a block away—turned almost condescending. "After you made that comment about reading tea leaves, I did a little research. No, it wasn't the kind of thing that was splashed all over the papers, but after I did a bit of digging, I found some interesting information about you and the way you've helped a couple of your neighbors here, like the woman who won some lottery money a few years back."

Exactly who had Lucy Margolis been talking to?

Well, probably anyone who would listen. I had no doubt she'd thought she was trying to help me by sending more tea-leaf-reading business my way, but right now, I really wished she hadn't been quite so zealous when it came to spreading the word about my supposed psychic abilities.

"Yes, I read tea leaves," I said. "That doesn't prove anything."

"No," Justin said reasonably. "But I saw your face when you got a good look at my gloves. You looked like you'd seen a ghost."

No, I thought, *only the face of the woman who'd tried to keep you from choking her to death.*

"You're admitting you killed Jessica Rosenthal?" I said next, a little surprised by my boldness. But then, he had me cornered, so it wasn't as though I had a lot to lose.

The halfway amused expression abruptly slipped from Justin's face. Now he just looked angry, his features hard and pinched at the same time, and I found myself wondering how I ever could have thought he was cute.

"I'm not admitting anything," he replied.

A few houses down from where we stood, someone opened their front door, showing a rectangle of warm yellow light.

Here was my chance.

"Help!" I yelled.

Or at least, that was the plan. Unfortunately, I didn't get out much more than "Hel—" before Justin clamped his hand on my mouth.

"Oh, no, you don't," he told me, his voice a harsh whisper in my ear.

I didn't even think. No, some primitive instinct made me bite down on the gloved hand that covered my lips, probably shredding the leather even further, and he let out a howl of pain and loosened his grip for a second.

That was the only opening I needed. I tore off down the street, legs pumping, and prayed he wasn't a very good runner. At once, he bolted after me, and I hastened my pace. We were only a quarter mile or so from the police station, and I figured that was my best chance of getting some help. Besides, I knew this neighborhood and Justin didn't, which meant I should be able to avail myself of a couple of helpfully placed alleyways and maybe lose him.

Even though I knew looking over my shoulder would only slow me down, I couldn't help risking a quick glance behind me. He was still a couple of yards away, and gaining fast.

Crap. I mustered every ounce of strength I possessed and told it to go straight to my feet. Back in high school, I'd been a pretty decent sprinter, even though I otherwise wasn't super athletic.

But it had been a long time since I'd had to run like this.

Scratch that. I'd never had to run for my life before.

And sure, maybe I could have taken to the air and escaped him that way, but I knew how important it was to center myself and maintain focus while I was using my magic, and I knew I sure as hell wouldn't be able to focus right now.

Besides, if I somehow managed to survive this encounter, I really didn't want a reputation as the coffee shop owner who could fly.

We were coming up on a corner, and I cut across it, angling toward the alleyway I knew lay behind the next street over. The slap of feet behind me told me that Justin definitely hadn't given up the pursuit, and in fact was gaining even more ground.

Which meant the alley wasn't such a great idea

after all, because he'd be able to see exactly where I was going.

Instead, I zigged to my right, heading back toward The Skillet. No, it wasn't the police station, but it was full of people, and right now, I had to believe there must be safety in numbers.

Justin was getting closer, though, and so I ran across the street, hoping my erratic movements might make it more difficult for him to figure out what I planned to do next.

But just as my feet touched the curb, lights flashed through the darkness, cutting across me before I heard a sickening thud and the screech of brakes. I stopped and turned to see what had happened.

Justin lay on the asphalt, shocked eyes staring up at the night sky. Just past him was a black and white Las Vegas P.D. cruiser, and Kyle climbing out of the driver's seat, his face pale. He was wearing jeans and a puffer jacket, telling me he'd definitely been off-duty when he got my text message.

"Is he...?" I asked, then stopped. While I couldn't help being almost sickeningly relieved by the way Kyle had come to the rescue, the last thing I wanted was for him to be responsible for anyone's death, even Justin Hale's.

Still looking way too white-faced, Kyle knelt down next to Justin and placed two fingers against his throat. "No, he's alive," he said. "Let me call an ambulance."

While I stood there, arms wrapped around myself as people began to emerge from their houses, coming out to see the source of the commotion on their quiet street, he leaned into the squad car so he could pick up the radio and call in the request. Just a moment or so later, sirens began to wail their way into the night.

Kyle came over and stood next to me until the ambulance arrived, and then informed the EMTs that the patient was also a suspect in a murder investigation, so he'd need to accompany them to the hospital. Before they left, though, he turned back toward me.

"Are you okay?" he asked.

I glanced over at Justin, who'd already been loaded into the back of the ambulance. He looked nearly as white as the sheet on the gurney beneath him, but I thought I saw his eyelids flutter, telling me he was starting to emerge from his faint. Still, it didn't look as though he'd be going anywhere any time soon.

"Yes," I said. "I'm okay."

It was the girl with the long brown hair—Cecily Mills—who eventually spilled the whole story. She and Justin had been seeing each other, and Jessica had found out and read him the riot act for having a relationship with a co-worker nearly fourteen years younger than he was.

That was the exact scenario my dream had shown me several days earlier...except at the time, I hadn't realized Justin was the one getting chewed out for his unprofessional behavior.

He'd told Jessica he was going to end the affair...only he hadn't. And when Jessica discovered that he'd been lying to her, she'd told him she was going to have him fired and make sure he'd never be able to work in TV again. Cecily claimed she had no clue that Justin had murder in his heart when he went to have it out with his co-producer, only that he was angry and wanted to talk her into changing her mind.

After hearing all this, I realized Justin had only asked me out to dinner that first time to provide himself with a sturdy alibi, since even the best forensic investigations couldn't pinpoint time of death to much more than forty-five minutes from the moment when it occurred. Since it sounded as though he'd headed right over to the Castañeda after the murder, he'd probably thought he had everything handled, that there was no way anyone could suspect him when he was out on a very public date with the gal who owned the town's most popular coffee shop.

Why he'd asked me out on a second date, I couldn't really say. Had he simply been trying to make sure his interest in me seemed genuine?

Maybe. And maybe the reason he and Cecily had been arguing on the street in front of the old cowboy emporium was that she'd found out about our second date and was giving Justin grief over it. She'd claimed over and over again that she hadn't been part of the scheme, and apparently the police believed her, because she hadn't been arrested as an accessory, had in fact been thanked for providing so much crucial information to the authorities.

"We still don't know if Justin really meant to kill Jessica Rosenthal," Kyle told me a few days later when he dropped into Levitation Latte for a midmorning pick-me-up, and to fill in some more details about exactly what had gone down. "Cecily made it sound as though he wanted to go and talk some sense into her, but Jessica wouldn't relent, and Justin lost his temper."

"You believe that?" I asked, not bothering to keep the dubious tone out of my voice. Most of the time, spur-of-the-moment acts of violence didn't include the suspect making sure he wore gloves and didn't leave any other physical evidence at the scene of the crime.

Well, other than those scraps of leather under Jessica's fingernails.

And then there was the little matter of him

using me as his alibi. He must have already known what he was planning, or I doubted he would have ever asked me to that first dinner at the Castañeda.

Kyle broke off a piece of banana-nut muffin and chewed it thoughtfully. "Doesn't really matter what I think," he said after he'd swallowed the morsel and washed it down with some cinnamon-spiced latte. "That's up to the jury, I suppose."

A trial date hadn't been set, mostly because Justin had suffered a broken leg and two fractured ribs after Kyle hit him with the squad car, so he wouldn't be out of the hospital for a while. But I had to believe when he did go to court, a jury would find the evidence pretty overwhelming.

"I suppose," I echoed, then added, "Thanks for coming to my rescue."

Kyle smiled and touched the badge he wore. "Just doing my job, ma'am."

I could only grin back at him, knowing he was teasing me a little. All the same, I didn't know what I would have done if he hadn't come careening around that corner, desperately trying to figure out where I'd gone. He'd told me he'd already gone around the block once, and it was sheer luck that he'd turned right then and caught Justin with the front bumper of his police cruiser.

Well, lucky for me, anyway.

Justin Hale would probably have a very different view of the situation.

Understandably, Justin's arrest threw the entire *Fix My Town* production into disarray. And because they'd only been a little more than a week into their renovations, the execs at the cable channel decided not to move forward with the Las Vegas episode, and pulled the plug on the whole thing.

But just as the Mackenzies—and Pastor Phil and the owners of the movie theater—were trying to figure out whether they could come up with the necessary funds to finish the various projects, Max stepped in and informed everyone that he would cover the cost of making sure everything was done, and done right. There had been a little bit of protest, but not much. No one else around here had his kind of deep pockets.

However, the Mackenzies did gift him with two of their prize horses as a way of saying thank-you for his financial support, which meant Max's stables were up and running a lot sooner than he'd expected. He had me over at his place to meet Sunset Ridge's latest additions, a sturdy quarter-horse gelding and a fun pinto mare who was an American Paint horse splashed in white and tan, and who gratefully accepted the apple I held out to her.

"Looks like she's going to be your horse," Max said with a grin.

"Well, I don't know about 'mine,'" I returned. "But I'm happy to ride her whenever you let me."

"It's a deal."

For a moment, we were silent. Then I commented, "Everyone's ready to give you the key to the city after what you did. Or is this your way of buttering up the citizens before you run for mayor?"

To my surprise, Max's expression turned serious. "There won't be another mayoral election for two years, so no, that wasn't really my motivation. But I did just tell my accountant to change my place of residence to New Mexico. I don't really see myself going back to L.A."

"You don't?" I responded, startled. Sure, Max had been spending a lot of time in Las Vegas lately, but it was still a big step from hanging out here in his spare time to making our little town his permanent residence.

"Nope," he said cheerfully. "I can catch a plane from here just as easily as I could in Southern California. Well, maybe not just as easily, but still, there's nothing about living in New Mexico that will get in the way of my filming schedule."

I had to admit that was true. At the same time, I wasn't sure whether I'd be able to sort out my tangled emotions upon hearing the news that Max wanted to make Las Vegas home again. As much as I missed him when he went away, his absence gave me the time I needed to maintain some emotional equilibrium.

"Anyway," he went on, "let's go for a ride."

"It's thirty-three degrees outside," I pointed out.

"Then it's not freezing, right?"

About all I could do was shake my head. But because it was Max, I said, "Yep—let's ride."

Two weeks after Justin Hale was taken to the hospital and the mystery of Jessica Rosenthal's death was solved, a letter came to the coffee shop. We didn't get much mail there, except utility bills and sales flyers, so I picked it up with some mystification and looked at the return address.

It was the address of an accounting firm in Los Angeles, which only increased my confusion. I'd never done business with anyone from L.A., so I couldn't figure out why the letter had come here.

I slid a fingernail under the flap and opened it. Inside were two pieces of paper: a short handwritten note...and a cashier's check for a hundred thousand dollars.

What the hell?

As Deanne hovered nearby, eyebrows lifted at the frown on my face, I unfolded the note.

If it weren't for you, I'd be in jail, and my

sister's killer would have gotten away with it. I just sold my grandparents' property, and I figure you've earned this. And don't try to send it back, because I'll just have my accountant cut you another check and mail it to you as many times as I have to.

Even though I didn't know Elliott Rosenthal very well, I could imagine him doing that very thing. And while I wasn't sure how to feel about taking the money, it seemed pretty clear to me that he wanted me to keep it.

Maybe I hadn't messed with the Powerball, but it sure looked like I'd just won my very own lottery.

"Hey," I said to Deanne, knowing exactly how I needed to spend some of that money.

"You want to go car shopping with me?"

Skye's adventures will continue in *Eclairs and Ectoplasm,* releasing in June 2023.

Also by Christine Pope

FAMILIAR SPIRITS

(Cozy Fantasy/Romance)

Spells and Spaniels (May 2023)

Cauldrons and Cats (August 2023)

Hexes and Hedgehogs (November 2023)

———

LATTES AND LEVITATION

(Cozy Mystery/Paranormal Romance)

Caffeine Before Curses

Muffins After Magic

Pastries and Prophecies

Eclairs and Ectoplasm

———

UNEXPECTED MAGIC*

(Urban Fantasy/Paranormal Romance)

Found Objects

Finders, Keepers

Lost and Found

Finding Destiny

HEDGEWITCH FOR HIRE

(Cozy Mystery/Paranormal Romance)

Grave Mistake

Social Medium

Household Demons

Perpetual Potion

Jingle Spells

Wandering Monsters

Uninvited Ghosts

Prophet Motive

Ballroom Bits

THE WITCHES OF WHEELER PARK*

(Paranormal Romance)

Storm Born

Thunder Road

Winds of Change

Mind Games

A Wheeler Park Christmas

Blood Ties

Healing Hands

Wishful Thinking

Smoke and Mirrors

MISS PRIMM'S ACADEMY FOR WAYWARD
WITCHES*

(Fantasy/Academy Romance)

Misspelled

Dispelled

Expelled

PROJECT DEMON HUNTERS*

(Paranormal Romance)

Unquiet Souls

Unbound Spirits

Unholy Ground

Unseen Voices

Unmarked Graves

Unbroken Vows

THE DEVIL YOU KNOW*

(Paranormal Romance)

Sympathy for the Devil

Charmed, I'm Sure

A Wing and a Prayer

Wish Upon a Star

THE WITCHES OF CANYON ROAD*

(Paranormal Romance)

Hidden Gifts

Darker Paths

Mysterious Ways

A Canyon Road Christmas

Demon Born

An Ill Wind

Higher Ground

Haunted Hearts

THE WITCHES OF CLEOPATRA HILL*

(Paranormal Romance)

Darkangel

Darknight

Darkmoon

Sympathetic Magic

Protector

Spellbound

A Cleopatra Hill Christmas

Impractical Magic

Strange Magic

The Arrangement

Defender

Bad Blood

Deep Magic

Darktide

THE DJINN WARS*

(Paranormal Romance)

Chosen

Taken

Fallen

Broken

Forsaken

Forbidden

Awoken

Illuminated

Stolen

Forgotten

Driven

Unspoken

THE WATCHERS TRILOGY*

(Paranormal Romance)

Falling Dark

Dead of Night

Rising Dawn

THE SEDONA FILES*

(Paranormal/Science Fiction Romance)

Bad Vibrations

Desert Hearts

Angel Fire

Star Crossed

Falling Angels

Enemy Mine

TALES OF THE LATTER KINGDOMS*

(Fantasy Romance)

All Fall Down

Dragon Rose

Binding Spell

Ashes of Roses

One Thousand Nights

Threads of Gold

The Wolf of Harrow Hall

Moon Dance

The Song of the Thrush

THE GAIAN CONSORTIUM SERIES*

(Science Fiction Romance)

Beast (free prequel novella)

Blood Will Tell

Breath of Life

The Gaia Gambit

The Mandala Maneuver

The Titan Trap

The Zhore Deception

The Refugee Ruse

STANDALONE TITLES

Hearts on Fire (Paranormal Romance)

Taking Dictation (Contemporary Romance)

Golden Heart (Gaslight Fantasy Romance)

Night Music: A Modern Reimagining of The Phantom of the Opera (Contemporary Romance)

Ghost Dance: A Sequel to Gaston Leroux's The Phantom of the Opera (Historical Mystery/Romance)

Flight Before Christmas (Fantasy Romance)

* Indicates a completed series

About the Author

USA Today bestselling author Christine Pope has been writing stories ever since she commandeered her family's Smith-Corona typewriter back in grade school. Her work includes paranormal romance, fantasy romance, and science fiction/space opera romance. She makes her home in beautiful Santa Fe, New Mexico.

 facebook.com/ChristinePopeAuthor

 twitter.com/ChristineJPope

 pinterest.com/ChristineJPope